Gandy Dancer

A student-led literary magazine of the State University of New York

Issue 13.2 | Spring 2025

gandy dancer /ˈgan dē ˌdans ər/ *noun*
1. a laborer in a railroad section gang that lays and maintains track. Origin: early 20th century: of unknown origin.

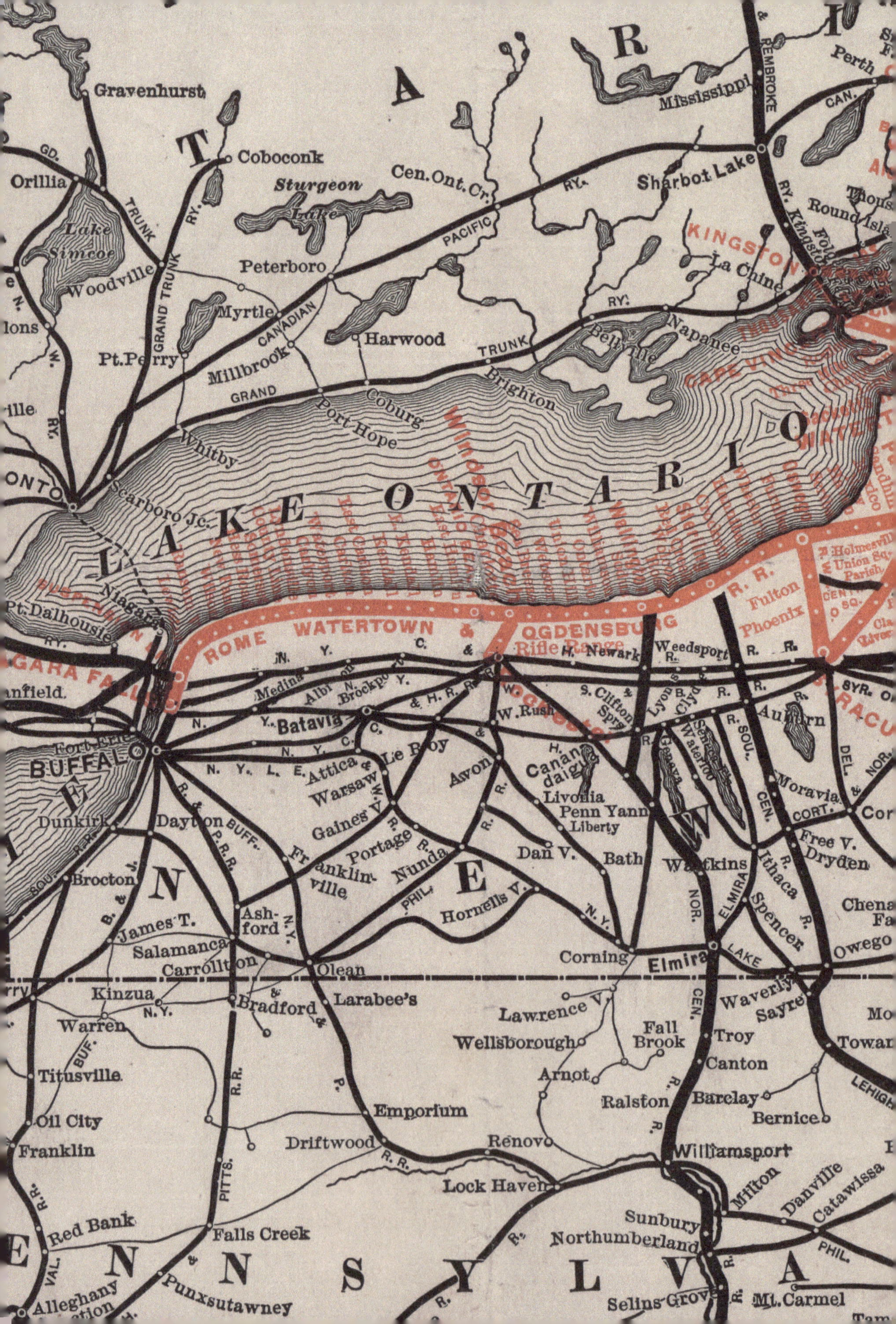

LAKE ONTARIO
Gravenhurst
Coboconk
Sturgeon Lake
Cen. Ont. Cr.
Mississippi
Sharbot Lake
Perth
Round Isla
Orillia
Lake Simcoe
Woodville
Peterboro
Myrtle
Harwood
La Chine
Napanee
Bellville
Pt. Perry
Millbrook
Brighton
Coburg
Port Hope
Whitby
Scarboro Jc.
KINGSTON
CAPE VINCENT
Niagara
Pt. Dalhousie
ROME WATERTOWN & OGDENSBURG R. R.
Rifle Range
Fulton
Phoenix
Newark
Weedsport
Medina
Albion
Brockport
Batavia
Fort Erie
BUFFALO
Attica
Le Roy
Warsaw
Avon
W. Rush
Clifton Sprs
Lyons
Canandaigua
Livonia
Penn Yann
Liberty
Auburn
Moravia
Dunkirk
Dayton
Gaines V.
Portage
Nunda
Dan V.
Bath
Watkins
Ithaca
Free V.
Dryden
Brocton
Franklinville
Hornells V.
Spencer
James T.
Ashford
Salamanca
Carrollton
Olean
Corning
Elmira
Owego
Kinzua
Bradford
Larabee's
Lawrence V.
Waverly
Sayre
Warren
Wellsborough
Fall Brook
Troy
Canton
Titusville
Arnot
Ralston
Barclay
Bernice
Oil City
Emporium
Franklin
Driftwood
Renovo
Williamsport
Lock Haven
Milton
Danville
Catawissa
Red Bank
Falls Creek
Sunbury
Northumberland
Punxsutawney
Selins Grove
Mt. Carmel
Alleghany

Ormstown
Rouse's Point
Moore's Jc.
Lacolle
Swanton Jc.
Huntingdon
Ft. Covington
St. Lawrence
MASSENA SPRS.
Sheldon Sprs.
Newport
Moira L.
Alburgh
Dickinson Cen.
St. Regis Falls
Shanley's
Santa Clara
Spring Cove
Chazy
Plattsburg
Chateaugay
Lyon Mtn.
Post Kent
Keeseville
Au Sable
St. Albans
BOSTON
Johnson
Essex Jc.
St. Johnsbury
LOWELL R. R.
Norwood Junc.
Potsdam
Canton
De Kalb Jc.
Richville
Gouverneur
Keene's
Hewerp
Philadelphia
FINE
Sterlingville
Harrisville
Natural Bridge
CARTHAGE
Deer River
Castor Land
LOWVILLE
Martinsburg
Glendale
Lyons Falls
Port Leyden
Leyden
BOONVILLE
Alder Cr.
TRENTON FALLS
Trenton
Holland Patent
Marcy
UTICA
ROME
W. Camden
Camden
Williams T.
Kasoag
Albion
Richland Jc.
Pierpont Manor
Adams Centre
Black River
Great Bend
Buck Mtn.
Paul Smith's
ADIRONDACK MTS.
Burlington
MONTPELIER
CEN. VER. R.
M. & W. R.
Wells Riv.
Northfield
Roxbury
Leicester Junction
Ft. Ticonderoga
Shroon Lake
Baldwin
Lake Champlain
Lake George
Castleton
North Creek
The Glen
Hudson
Caldwell
Whitehall
Rutland
White Riv. Jc.
BOSTON
Connecticut R.
Claremont
Glen's Falls
Ft. Edward
North V.
Bellows Falls
Ilion
Herkimer
Little Falls
St. Johns V.
Ft. Plain
Johns T.
Glovers V.
Saratoga Sprs
Petersburg Jc.
Keene
Manchester
Oneida
Clinton
Fonda
Amsterdam
Ballston
Pownal
North Adams
Grouts Cor.
Greenfield
CHES. R. R.
Fitchburg
FITCHBURG R.
Richfield Sprs.
Rotterdam Junc.
Schenectady
Troy
ALBANY
Earlville
Schuyler Lake
Otsego Lake
Norwich
Coopers T.
Sharon Sprs.
Chatham
State Line
Pittsfield
Worcester
Sidney
SUSQ.
Cobleskill
Colliers
CATSKILL MTS.
Hudson
BOSTON & ALBANY
Westfield
Springfield
Palmer
Binghamton
Tivoli
Enfield
PROVIDENCE R. I.
Great Bend
WESTN.
Delaware
Rhinebeck
HOUSATONIC
HARTFORD
NEW YORK CENTRAL
Poughkeepsie
Lackawaxen
Newburgh
Fishkill
Middletown
Scranton
Middle T.
Garrisons
Saybrook
New London
Norwich
Port Jervis
Peekskill
Sing Sing
Tarry T.
New Haven
Bridgeport
Wilkesbarre
White Haven
Manunka Chunk
Washington
Jersey City
Paterson
Penn Haven
Mauch Chunk
Den V.
NEW YORK
LONG ISLD.
VERMONT
NEW HAMPSHIRE
MASS.
CONN.
NEW YORK

gandy dancer /ˈɡan dē ˌdans ər/ *noun* **1.** a laborer in a railroad section gang that lays and maintains track. Origin: early 20th century: of unknown origin.

We've titled our journal *Gandy Dancer* after the slang term for the railroad workers who laid and maintained the railroad tracks before the advent of machines to do this work. Most theories suggest that this term arose from the dance-like movements of the workers, as they pounded and lifted to keep tracks aligned. This was grueling work, which required the gandy dancers to endure heat and cold, rain and snow. Like the gandy dancers, writers and artists arrange and rearrange, adjust and polish to create something that allows others passage. We invite submissions that forge connections between people and places and, like the railroad, bring news of the world.

Gandy Dancer is published biannually in the spring and fall by the State University of New York College at Geneseo. Issues of *Gandy Dancer* are freely available for view or download from gandydancer.org, and print copies are available for purchase. Special thanks to the College at Geneseo's Department of English and Milne Library for their support of this publication.

ISSN: 2326-439X

ISBN (THIS ISSUE): 978-1-956862-12-6

We publish writing and visual art by current students and alumni of the State University of New York (SUNY) campuses only.

Our Postscript section features work by SUNY alumni. We welcome nominations from faculty and students as well as direct submissions from alumni themselves. Faculty can email Rachel Hall, faculty advisor, at hall@geneseo.edu with the name and email address for the alum they wish to nominate, and alums can submit through our website. Both nominations and direct submissions should indicate which SUNY the writer attended, provide a graduation date, and the name and email of a faculty member we can contact for confirmation.

We use Submittable to manage submissions and the editorial process. Prospective authors can submit at gandydancer.submittable.com/submit. Please use your SUNY email address for your user account and all correspondence.

Gandy Dancer will accept up to three submissions from an author at a time.

FICTION: We accept submissions up to 25 pages. Stories must be double-spaced. We are unlikely to accept genre or fan-fiction.

CREATIVE NONFICTION: We accept submissions up to 25 pages. CNF must be double-spaced.

POETRY: Three to five poems equal one submission. Poems must be submitted as a single document. Format as you would like to see them in print. Our text columns are generally 4.5 inches wide, at 11pt font.

VISUAL ART: We accept submissions of art—especially photos, drawings, and paintings—in the file formats jpeg, tiff, and png. Submitted images should have a minimum resolution of 300 dpi and be at least 5 inches wide. Please include work titles and mediums in your submissions.

Please visit us at www.gandydancer.org, or scan the qr code below.

Questions or comments? Send us an email at gandydancer@geneseo.edu

GENESEO | Milne Library

Special thanks to: the Parry family and Amy Stuber

Dear Readers,

As the door to our college careers begins to close, we look back at our work on *Gandy Dancer's* staff with enormous gratitude. This particular issue feels just as special as the previous one, it being our last. We want to thank our fellow staff members, all of our wonderful contributors, and you, dearest reader.

This semester we had the incredible opportunity to interview Amy Stuber after reading her debut short story collection, *Sad Grownups*. This collection features stories that explore the winding paths and raw transformations of becoming, and being, an adult. You will find both a review of her collection and the interview in the back of this issue. (Something we hope you enjoy!)

We were fortunate to receive a significant number of really strong art submissions this semester, with an abundance coming from the Fashion Institute of Technology, and each piece selected tugs on a different emotional chord. Desislava Furber's "Necrolog (10 Years)" addresses mourning rituals in Bulgaria that continue forty days, a year, or even ten years after the death of a loved one. Sara Aparicio's "Empanadas" evokes a deep sense of joy through the use of bright paint swatches. Some of the artwork takes us to uncomfortable places, like "Immaculate Conception" by Alex Herrera, which suggests a certain intimacy with the natural world. We've also been delighted by the various mediums and methods artists have utilized this semester.

So much poetry in this semester is evocative and sure-footed, as well. Zoe LaVallee writes: "Tulips burst / from sticky stems and bend ever / so slightly over the marigold patch" and in Magdalene Joseph's "Reef is Just a Synonym for Heaven," the speaker wishes to "kiss [their] brother's cool cheek one last time." Alternatively, Ada Benedicto's "Sunday Brunch" provides a sharp, clear-eyed view of the stain of consumerism and American nationalism, ending with the lines: "I'm Red 40 glow. / I'm an American."

In Amelia Weitknecht's "Imagination's Memoir," imagination is the narrator who invites us to recall the pleasures of childlike curiosity and creativity. As we grow up we tend to grow apart, but our imagination never forgets us; and like old friends, we are reminded that we can still visit each other as if nothing has changed.

Every piece in this issue has been shaped by the creative minds of our wonderful authors and artists. We invite you to get back in touch with your imagination as you travel through this issue.

This goodbye is bittersweet, though our joy is overshadowed by our sadness. It has been a tremendous pleasure working as Managing Editors for the

2024-25 year, and we feel extremely confident that the magazine has been left in good hands. Join us on our last journey through *Gandy Dancer*.

Onwards!
Mollie McMullan and Jordyn Stinar

Table of Contents

COVER ART: elbow room (oil on canvas), Jade Maracic

NATALIE MCKENZIE

My Family's Hands

Dad's hands are like a worn baseball glove. Dry, cracked, and abused, his palms expand into meaty digits weathered by a life on the farm and upstate winters. His fingernails are dark and fractured, broken like the wood chips at the playground. His hands have turned to leather, dried and stretched by years of labor. I imagine my dad lathering lotion into the pits and ravines of his skin, the moisture sinking deeper and deeper until it disappears off the cliffs. Dad would come in from the barn and place his icy mitts against my neck, sending shivers up my spine. I suppose his hands have become numb to the elements. Whenever I think about the kind of man my father is, I think about his hands, a testament to his work ethic and humbleness.

Mom's hands stretch forever like saltwater taffy spinning on a wheel at a fair. Her fingers extend from looming palms, reaching like spider legs or jellyfish tentacles. Calluses poke out where finger meets palm, hardened from riding horses and doing pull-ups in the gym. I picture her in the gymnasium of the same high school I attended palming a basketball. She'd strut over to where the boys were shooting hoops, cross them up, and swish the net in their faces. I'm sure one of the guys would make a comment about a woman's ball and chuck a man's at her chest. Her ready hands would snatch it from the air, dribble with ease, and drain a bucket with a devilish grin. Her hands were designed for athleticism. For wrapping around a softball bat or flicking a basketball in a soaring arch to the backboard. Mom's hands reject the dainty expectations of femininity. When I think of my mom, her hands remind me of her power and strength.

Grandma's hands bend and twist, morphed by the cruelty of time. Once straight and long, now crooked and bulged like knots in a tree. Veins run like rivers of life, poking against wrinkled skin, weaving a tapestry of blue. Her hands used to expand as far as Mom's, but gravity stunted and pressed his might against the once-long lines. I imagine Grandma threading a needle, misshapen fingers shaking slightly but still managing to slip the elusive thread through the tiny hole. Grandma would yell at the Yankees on the television while hand-stitching the border of the next quilt to be sold or gifted to the friend or family member she deemed worthy of her precious work. I suppose this work would have been swift and painless before age took her hands hostage, but now I can only guess the aches in her joints as she pushes the needle through fabric and repeats the in-out motion like rising and crashing waves. When I think of my grandma, I think of her knobby knuckles weaving love into her creations.

My hands are small. They lack the stretching fingers of my mom or the thick wide palms of my dad. My hands are smooth, without calluses or cracks from cold New York winters. My hands look nothing like my parents'. Maybe one day they will be bent and twisted like Grandma's from typing at a computer or plucking out notes on ivory for the songs I sing. I hide my hands from Mom and Dad, ashamed mine don't tell a story like the ones I see written on their skin. My hands don't speak of hard work. My hands don't speak of days on a court or field. My hands don't speak of hours spent with a sewing machine. What story do my hands tell? I imagine years down the road, my daughter might grab my hand in her soft pink clutch and trace my veins and lines like roads on a map. I hope one day my daughter sees Dad's dedication, Mom's strength, and Grandma's generosity etched into the storybook of my skin.

JENNA CURTIS

Syllabus Week

A found poem after my notes

I.
Smells of sleep and autonomy.
Storytelling—think deeply: somber,
blunt, sovereignty, and export project.
Social geography—15 facts about myself—
pretended to be someone else.
Enchantment. Purple. Fitted for you.
Smells of autonomy, a collection of
have-to-be's.

II.
De-mythologizing the schedule.
Final project—advanced—rambling
and unclear. Failure student does not
meet the requirements,
10% *No late credit.*
Intellectual Integrity.
60% *No late credit.*

III.
Exit West,
rambling and unclear, significance
of the narrative. *There, There.*

The Street Cat

I met a cat on the street today.
She was a long-haired tortoiseshell cat
(which she insisted was wrong
as tortoises were nothing like her
for they have no hair at all?!).

So, I asked her,
"What'd you rather I call you?"
and she pondered for a moment.
Pink and black toe pads rose
from the sidewalk and scratched
at the sooted daub on her nose.
"I cannot say what for sure."

She continued,
"What do you think would be fitting?"
I watched her spin in slow circles,
her apricot eyes' black pits expand,
looking up and down at her mottled
splodges of sun and shadow fur.

"Maybe you're a dusk-smudged cat?"
Her head tilted, asking for elaboration.
"Well, I guess cause your fur
is painted all dusk-ish.
And looking like the sky and the clouds
after the sun disappears, I mean."

“I do like that—very much, in fact,”
she added after a moment of consideration.
Then, she kept slinking down the sidewalk
and brushed her oil-painted-horizon
against the pant leg of my dirty blue jeans.

MAGDALENE JOSEPH

Reef is Just a Synonym for Heaven

My brother died on the 8th that year
They said when he was little, he loved swimming
I imagine him as a fish, every now and again
Some beautiful rainbow trout with gaping lips
Or maybe a harmonious koi fish with whiskers
So now the sea hums, every time I walk close
Inviting me to dip my fingertips in
And maybe kiss my brother's cool cheek one last time.

Quinceañera (collagraph), Luissed Yibirin

Introspection of a Memory (monotype and screenprint), Luissed Yibirin

JULIA GARTLEY

The Supplicant

I saw Ruth for the first time in math class. She sat in front of me, and I spent an entire class watching her absently braid and re-braid her long, cornsilk hair. Later, I found myself beseeching God over my lunch tray.

I had transferred to St. Mary's School for Girls a month into my sophomore year of high school because my parents had decided that they wanted me to be friends with a different sort of girl than I had been friends with at my public school. My best friend and I had not had the right sort of friendship. A St. Mary's girl, they said, wouldn't cross the same lines.

It wasn't in that math class that Ruth and I became friends. We were assigned to work on an English project together and made a poster about *Romeo and Juliet.* She spent an entire class period writing the title of the play in big, neat, bubble letters on the top of the poster as I helpfully detailed, in a comedy-club manner, everything that Shakespeare had done wrong. I incredulously mocked the melodrama, age gap, and the notion that anyone could fall in love so quickly. Ruth laughed like I was Steve Martin. We had spent so much time on the lettering (her, writing; me, monologuing) that the rest of the poster had to be scribbled out at the last minute. We got a C+, if I recall, but she asked me to come over to her house that weekend.

I don't remember anything about the first time, or the second, or the third, but I was soon being hugged by her mom every time I came over and asked by her dad how my last softball game went. I was being invited to stay for dinner and had inside jokes with her older brother.

My parents loved her. When she came over to my house for the first time, she wore a gold cross on a delicate gold chain around her neck that she would unconsciously fiddle with from time to time (I had never seen the necklace before). She told them about her confirmation classes and bashfully agreed to pray over dinner, which immediately erased the semi-permanent creases in their brows. Ruth winked at me whenever they weren't looking. After she left, my parents told me that she was exactly the kind of girl they had hoped I would become friends with at St. Mary's.

When I went to her house, Ruth would take my hand the minute I had my shoes off and pull me upstairs to her bedroom, where we would flop unceremoniously onto her bed. If I were going over to her house after school, I would spend hours thinking of things she might find funny and how I would say them. Then I would perform, like a player at the Globe, and she would laugh until tears came out of her eyes, which was when I knew I had prepared a particularly good set.

We would talk too, mostly about boys. Ruth liked this boy named Nick from the boys' school, and everyone knew that he liked her back. They hung out a lot in that high school way: not together but not *not* together, tentatively holding hands in movie theaters, maintaining the pointless charade, when they were teased, that they were just good friends and had no idea why people thought otherwise. She didn't waste the charade on me. She told me about his eyes and his hair and that she thought he was working up to ask her to be his girlfriend. She told me about the time he had kissed her at the joint homecoming hosted in the shared gym at the girls' school and how his face had gone red, which she thought was cute.

One time, she asked me who I liked, and I chose Nick's friend Liam. This made Ruth squeal with excitement, and she decided that us becoming their girlfriends was a foregone conclusion. She proclaimed that we would go to their games together (they were on the volleyball team) and when they won, they would come running over to us and kiss us triumphantly on the lips, and we, of course, would love it, but would pretend to be grossed out by how sweaty they were. They would laugh at us for being so squeamish (that's just how girls are, they would say), then kiss us again before running back to celebrate with their team.

Ruth animated her fantasy with an urgent sense of excitement, and in that moment, I couldn't remember having ever wanted something so badly. So, as girls do, we giggled and giggled and squealed and squealed, and she emphatically put her hand on my thigh, which gave my laugh a bit of a hysterical edge.

Two weeks after Ruth and Nick started dating, Ruth told me I should come to a party at Nick's house, implying not-so-subtly that Liam had told her he wanted me there. I came over to her house before, and she squawked indignantly when she realized that I didn't intend to wear any makeup. She pulled me onto her bedroom floor and cupped my chin with her hand as she carefully dabbed red lipstick from her mom's makeup bag onto my bottom lip with her middle finger, then told me to rub my lips together, miming the action with her own reddened lips. She laughed when I tried to do as she said, then grabbed the back of my neck and pressed her mouth to mine because I couldn't be trusted to do it properly, she said. She laughed at my surprise. Ruth actually laughed like people did in cartoons and movies, with her head thrown mirthfully back and her hands clutching her stomach as though her sides had split and she was trying to keep her organs from spilling out. I tried to imitate her laugh and tentatively touched my fingers to my mouth, which had begun to burn.

There weren't many people at Nick's house, and in fact, I was the only person there who had been invited by someone other than Nick. When we got there, he nodded to me and casually slung his arm across Ruth's shoulders. Ruth unsubtly gestured with a tilt of her head at Liam, who had been watching us since we came in. I shrugged vaguely. She smiled and winked as Nick led her away, presumably to some dark, unpeopled corner.

I don't remember the chain of events that led to Liam's hot mouth clumsily covering mine or his damp palms fumbling with the hem of the shirt that Ruth had lent me as we sat, completely alone, on a stained couch in Nick's basement, but I find them irrelevant anyway. I had spent so many hours in Ruth's bedroom, sprawled on her soft, carpeted floor or shoulder-to-shoulder with her in her twin bed, listening to her try and interpret Nick's actions and text messages like they were lines on an ancient, archaic scroll: inscrutable, enigmatic, ambiguous. But I ended up being kissed and touched by a boy for the same unambiguous reasons that Juliet and Eve and Helen had: merely for having skin and hair and warm blood.

Still, he kissed me with an unfeigned earnestness that made me pity him, and when he pulled away, he wasn't Romeo or Adam or Paris. He was just a boy with wide, uncertain eyes and a smear of red lipstick on his chin who had been told that the thing to do at a party was kiss a girl.

He tentatively, almost reluctantly, reached for me again, but I pulled away this time. "You don't have to."

His nod seemed more like an involuntary twitch, and he fell back, looking almost relieved, into the cushions of the couch.

We were silent for a moment. "Was that your first kiss?" he asked after a while, his voice a little raspy.

"No." With my fingernail, I picked at the seam of the couch cushion under me.

"Oh. It was mine." He looked down.

We were silent again. He was still looking away from me, but I studied his profile. Without thinking, I wet my thumb and started wiping at the lipstick on his chin. He looked confused, but let me do it. Even after it was gone, the residue left his skin pink.

Liam gave me a little smile. We stayed side-by-side on the couch until it was time to leave.

I slept at Ruth's house that night. She demanded details and bit her lip with excitement when I told her that Liam had kissed me. She asked me if I liked it, and I told her that I had. She buried her head in her pillow to stifle her giggles when I asked where she and Nick had gone off to, and she told me, between peals of incredulous laughter, how he had folded her shirt and jeans after taking them off, how he had made strange faces when she touched him (she reenacted these for me), how he had held her afterward like she was something unbelievably precious. At this, she blushed wildly and smiled in an unrestrained, thoughtlessly happy way.

I lay awake all night trying desperately not to feel the arm that Ruth had carelessly thrown across my stomach. My own arm lay flat on the bed next to me, as if glued or bolted. It was like lying next to a live wire. Her gentle snores sounded electric.

My parents suggested that I bring her to my church's fall camp that year. The camp was on a lake and populated with a handful of mismatched buildings that seemed like they had been strewn about in a haphazard game of marbles. Ruth was, as she always was, instantly charmed, remarking on how blue the lake was and how delightfully unlike a church the quaint little chapel seemed (it looked closer to a barn than a house of worship, with its hard-packed dirt floor and the fact that it had been, apparently, hastily constructed from half-rotted wood. But the planks that made up the roof had long since separated, so on sunny days, rays of sun were remarkably filtered through the slats in a way that immediately recalled divinity, which I always thought made it an uncommonly appropriate place for services to be held).

When I had asked her, she'd looked at me in the way that I'd become used to being looked at whenever I brought up anything related to church or God: With the usual wary, apprehensive grimace that seemed to be anticipating judgment. Her family was religious too, but to her, faith was like a coat that could be shed when it got too warm, or a costume that could be donned for the right occasion, then put back into the closet to be forgotten for a while, or so it seemed to me.

Mine clung to me, but it was beginning to lose its tack. Every time I saw Ruth, the fires seemed to burn a bit brighter, and I couldn't decide which was more terrifying: that the kingdom of God didn't exist, or that it did, and I would be denied entry.

A road ran through the camp, and on one side was a hill, and on the other, the lake. Our cabin was one of the only ones next to the lake, which made us feel deliciously separate. The cabin had a long hallway running down the center of it, off of which were individual bedrooms that had two or three bunk beds each. There was one outlier at the end of the hall that curiously had only a full bed, which Ruth quickly claimed for the two of us, telling the other girls that we were used to it. I smiled with great effort and prepared myself for a few more sleepless nights.

I could immediately tell that Ruth liked our counselor. I knew Olivia from church, and was proud to be able to present her to Ruth as an acceptable specimen from my world. She was pretty and bright and played soccer at the prestigious liberal arts college she attended, and her presence seemed like sufficient confirmation to Ruth that the weekend would be free of the usual horrors of religion, like crucifixes and brimstone. To my relief, she relaxed perceptibly after the introduction.

There were services in the chapel twice a day, which Ruth clearly thought was excessive. She complained in loud whispers all the way through the first morning service, and finally lay her head dramatically on my shoulder and pretended to fall asleep, disturbing the escaped pieces of hair from my ponytail with her uneven breaths. It was the typical purity sermon: A few times throughout, the pastor would say something that would cause her breath to hitch or would make her squirm a little against my shoulder like a fussy child.

Afterward, we were free to do whatever we wanted. I knew a lot of the other kids there and was friends with a few of them, but Ruth pulled me away to the lake, saying that she wanted to go swimming.

Despite the heat of the day, we were miraculously the only ones there. We could hear the distant shouts of those playing volleyball or foursquare on the courts by the cabins, but the hill across the road may as well have been another world.

I was sitting on the dock, leaning back on the palms of my hands, feet dipping languidly in and out of the water. Ruth was floating on her back, her face utterly serene, her golden hair forming a halo around her head, which made her look like a saint in effigy, or perhaps Ophelia. Both of these images disturbed me, and I tried to put them out of my mind.

After a while, she swam over to where I sat, then folded her arms up on the dock and rested her head on them. Her hair was darkened with water and her skin was beaded intricately with glassy droplets. Sometimes, I thought half-hysterically, she didn't seem real.

She stared at me pensively for a few minutes before I said, "What, Weirdo?" with a smile I hoped was casual.

She smacked my thigh with the back of her hand, then said with a consciously defiant look, "I'm not sorry about what happened with Nick."

Despite my best efforts, I couldn't forget what she had told me the night of the party. I knew that she was talking about whatever the two of them had done when they disappeared to Nick's bedroom. I fought against the image of his hands on her, and fought even harder against wondering what it was like.

Slightly stricken, I made sure she saw me roll my eyes. "Okay, nobody's asking you to be sorry." We were both seasoned Catholic school girls, so we both knew that this wasn't strictly true, but she seemed to allow herself to be reassured by my words, and the grave expression fell from her face as she laughed, throwing her glistening head back in that careless way of hers.

"I swear to God I saw that pastor look me dead in the eyes like, six times." She pushed off from the dock and started treading water in front of me, her long, pale legs suspended easily beneath the surface.

I scoffed. "I don't know what you could've possibly seen with your eyes closed for the whole sermon." I knew that she hadn't actually been asleep, but I played along anyway, reading the lines that she wanted me to read.

She splashed water onto my lap in a show of righteous indignation. "I'm just naturally very intuitive. I could *feel* his eyes." It was an effort to hold back the rueful laugh that had risen suddenly in my throat.

"You want to know what I think?" I said, now singularly focused on my thighs. I feverishly noted the beginnings of a sunburn.

"More than anything," she replied with a sweet smile as she swam back over to me, wrapping her hands beseechingly around the tops of my thighs and forcing me to look at her again. I fought to remember what I had been about to say.

"You tend to believe that people think about you way more than they actually do," I said after a moment, feeling a little smug at how bitingly insightful I thought I sounded. I had noticed that she always seemed to assume that people were concerned with what she was doing. It often seemed, in fact, that she wanted them to be.

Ruth wasn't offended like most people might have been. She never was. She only smiled bigger and said, "I bet *you* think about me." Any ounce of smugness I had felt a moment ago vanished, and my ears began to feel hot. Resting her chin on my knees, Ruth gave me a look full of mischief and terrible significance. "I swear that you can feel someone's eyes on you," she said, then laughed heartily like she had made a great joke. I couldn't look at her. Sometimes it felt like she knew everything.

Because Ruth had braided her hair after we'd left the lake, it was still wet during the evening service and it dripped periodically onto the cracked wooden pew.

I don't remember what the service was about, but I remember that the expression on Ruth's face kept oscillating between hysterical amusement and carefully disguised shame. I could always tell when Ruth was trying to hide something like this, because she covered it with this strange, dry smile. Still, she giggled her way through most of the service and even buried her face in my shoulder a few times to muffle her laughter. I had a wet spot on my shirt by the time it was over. After our conversation on the dock, I felt alarmingly naked. I couldn't seem to find anything to say to her, and I didn't even jokingly reprimand her for her rudeness like I might have done otherwise. Ruth didn't seem to notice my silence.

After the band (whose performance Ruth loved to mock, particularly the boyishly warbly voice of the lead singer) had finished their final song, Olivia took us and our cabin-mates to do "group time" under the canopy of a large pine tree. The sun had been down for hours, and everyone's faces were eerily illuminated by her lantern. We were supposed to discuss the sermon, but the allotted time tended to devolve into group confessions, with Olivia playing her part of the solemn but nonjudgmental priest. Ruth liked Olivia, and I could tell that even she was somewhat taken with her hieratic airs. Something about the dark and the hour and the reassuringly ordinary sight of Olivia's chipped pink nail polish and beatific expression on her face led girls to tearfully confess to lies they had told, people they had hurt, and things they had done with their boyfriends. Ruth didn't participate, but she watched the proceedings closely, and once even leaned in as if to say something before quickly withdrawing.

Olivia woke us up the next morning before the sun rose and ushered us outside to a firepit. Campers from the surrounding lakeside cabins stood around awkwardly, some leaning against each other like trees, others determinedly rubbing the sleep from their eyes. Ruth made to grab my arm to pull herself into my side, but I gently shook her off. She tilted her head at me, clearly confused, but I just shrugged at her.

The counselors did this every year. They woke us up in the middle of the night and had us all hold hands around the fire while one of them artlessly strummed the chords to some hymn on an acoustic guitar. With all of us singing and swaying and illuminated fiercely in the firelight (Olivia looked particularly otherworldly, her eyes closed and her lips moving rapidly as if she had become the earthly mouthpiece of some unseen, divine entity), it felt as though we were performing some pagan ritual. Ruth was holding my hand. The hymn was one we often sang before class in school, and I saw out of the corner of my eye that Ruth's lips formed the words as she swayed with the group, apparently somewhat caught up in the ritual's strange, hypnotic power.

"What the actual hell was that, Paige?" she asked once we were back inside. I sat on the bed, and she flopped down next to me and let out an exaggerated yawn. "I mean, that was some *cult* shit," she said, but her eyes were still a little glazed over. She hoisted herself up onto her elbows and looked over at me, finally seeming to note my silence. "Also, you've been weird all day. You basically tried to shove me into the fire when I touched your arm outside."

I shot her what I hoped was a scathing look. "No I didn't."

"Yeah, I'm pretty sure you did." She reached over and pushed me down into the bed so that we were about eye level. She kept her hand on my sternum.

"Why are you always doing this?" I said abruptly, still turning our conversation at the lake over and over in my mind. I put my hand over hers to show her what I meant. Sometimes, it felt like she knew exactly what she was doing when she touched me in her proprietary way. I often felt that I was a toy being batted between the paws of a cat, but there were moments when I allowed myself to think that it wasn't a game or an act. Sometimes, I allowed myself to think that we wanted the same thing.

The part of me that spoke was going rogue, as if it was acting without the permission of the whole. Even as the words left my lips, I felt as though I was committing a violation. In that moment, we were Adam and Eve, suddenly and shamefully aware of our nakedness. At some point, we had silently agreed to pile all the unspoken things on top of ourselves until, apparently, one of us started to fracture under the weight.

Ruth looked stricken. She pulled her hand from my sternum and turned onto her side without another word. She spent the night facing away from me and I spent the night bitterly regretting my moment of insanity.

Ruth wasn't there when I woke up, only a divot in the mattress where she had slept. I found her sitting at a table in the dining hall, deep in conversation with Olivia. I went up to them, and Ruth greeted me cheerfully, going on about how tired she was and how much she missed Nick and how the pancakes they were serving up weren't half bad, actually, as long as you put enough syrup on them. I nodded absently, suddenly feeling as though I could cry.

It was a beautiful day, and rays of sun reached into the old chapel like great, heavenly fingers. Ruth maneuvered Olivia to sit between us. She talked animatedly to both Olivia and I until the service started, even making a show of cajoling me into doing my impression of our math teacher for Olivia, but there was an almost aloof politeness to her tone when she addressed me that made it clear that something had come to an end.

Ruth didn't laugh at all during the sermon. The pastor spoke about David and Bathsheba, about willfully taking what it is unwholesome to covet, and called for all those who were burdened with sin to come forward and receive prayer from the present counselors. Ruth rose immediately with the drove, many of whom were beginning to shake with sobs, and kneeled before the pulpit. With distant horror I realized Ruth was crying, and her form became, for a moment, indistinguishable from the undulating mass of sinners at the front of the room. Olivia went to her, her face limned with divine ecstasy, and laid her hand beneficently on her brow. The image reminded me of an old statue of Mary that stood inconveniently in the math wing of our school. The statue's head was wreathed in a stony halo, and her hand was laid on the repentant brow of a faceless, kneeling supplicant. Last spring, someone painted Mary's toenails a bright, matchbox car red, and the nuns had been all in an uproar. Ruth didn't have to tell me that she had done it; every time someone brought it up or the nuns tried to intimidate us into confessing, her eyes glimmered with illicit pride.

But now, she was the perfect supplicant, just as imagined by the sculptor. I try not to remember her as she was in that moment, head bowed, eyes all red, form being covetously grasped by the godly sunbeams that had infiltrated the chapel, but no matter how many years pass, I can't seem to erase it from my mind.

When we returned home, Ruth took up with Nick as if nothing had changed, and I found that I had spent all my time at St. Mary's so utterly wrapped up in her that I hadn't made any other friends. Instead of whispering to Ruth during my classes, I began to look around and realize that I didn't know many of my classmates' names. It was like a spell had been broken and my ball gown had finally turned back into rags.

I made new friends at school. They were the kind of girls my parents didn't think would be a problem at St. Mary's.

I still saw Ruth in class. She never took off the gold cross necklace now, and I wondered if it had become permanently fused to her skin. She didn't talk to me anymore, but sometimes I would turn around in class and catch her staring at me. It was the kind of stare that's so intense, it's almost embarrassing to witness. Our eyes would meet for a single, agonizing moment before she would look away, as if to hide her reddening face.

Too Good (oil on canvas), Alexandra Cordato

CATIE MCGUIRE

Canned Artichoke Hearts

At the age of fifteen
your father took you home
to the five acres
and light blue aluminum
barn. In the kitchen
he opened the cabinet
old, cold toned
wood, and grabbed the cans
wrapped in unsaturated green
and yellow labels. Carrots
and green beans. Corn and
over-sized yam cans.
There's no way to know
what's in the ones that have
lost their labels. They've
lived long in that cabinet. His
mother's cabinet
of expired things.
One by one, he puts them
on the formica.
Tin clacking
on contact. Looking
at the expiration dates stamped
on their lids,

he laughed
and said ‘some of these
are older than you.’
1994, 1998
‘What year were you
born in again?’
You remain seated on
the stool. You tell him
the date. He nods, pretending
to remember a newborn
in a hospital room.
‘Wow!
it’s really been that long, huh?’
He almost sounds
impressed with himself.

CATIE MCGUIRE

Lessons of Faint Montana

I roll back into Arizona, single and pale
unfolding the delphiniums into porcelain

deep heat, white flower—

I believed in cracking webs into the ceramic sink
before finding remedy in Montana pastures.

I forgave your making of my hummingbird skin
blue petals blurring the tender green layer.

I let longing dehydrate in clay-basin appetite,
wild mustard water hardening into honey,
bruises healing, bitter sweetening.

—I returned to Arizona;   delphiniums unfolded,   china petrified.
You stared from the porch;   kiln knuckles curled,   temper
unchanged.

CATIE MCGUIRE

LAMENT

I SIT IN THE CHURCH:
prayer against my father's
abuse of the blood.

I SWAY IN THE BASEMENT:
elevator pale drink
down my throat.

A photograph sobers the splits in my skin
I hope my mouth doesn't move like his.

MIA PAONE

The Stillness We Share

You move like night—deadly quiet, yet soft and delicate, stitched into the fabric of the shadows. I didn't expect to meet you out here, not in the deepest and darkest hour of the evening, not on this cracked sidewalk, where the streetlights hum and flicker and the black ice glides under my sneakers. But here you are, mid-step, your doll-like eyes gleaming black and watery under the moonlight, caught somewhere between running and standing still. If you were a fellow Homo sapiens comrade of the night, another soul with opposable thumbs wandering between here and there, caught after hours in the time of night when nothing good can come of anything, then maybe this would be awkward. Maybe I would have crossed the street. Or maybe stared at my shoelaces, or pretended to be in a great hurry, or smiled a tight-lipped smile with a slight nod in your direction.

Instead, I almost apologize for being here, and I worry that I am disturbing whatever moonlit mission you were on. Instead, I just stand here, breath fogging in the cold, waiting for your eyes to blink, for your ear to twitch, for your tail to flicker, or for your feet, dressed in the most elegant of gleaming black, to shift. But you stand frozen. Unmoving. And so do I.

"It's nice to meet you," I say. But maybe introductions are pointless, because perhaps you already know me. Maybe you have seen people like me many times before. Have been hunted by someone like me. Have watched people like me stalk home after doing God knows what, tiptoeing through the streets like a bandit, hoping that the moon won't tell anyone our secrets.

I am certain that I know you. Oh, yes, I have seen you before. I have seen your brothers and sisters with bloated bellies and bulging eyes and lolling tongues, smeared on the side of the road in rainbows of red and black and brown. I have seen your fathers above fireplaces, with still-soft fur and glass eyes that are forever open. I have seen photos of you, being held up by your antlers as you lay slumped on the forest floor. I have seen you strung up by your spindly legs like piñatas, your warm belly sliced open in a straight line made by a sharp knife, your steaming innards pooled around them. My mother spoke to me of you, whispering to me in the late hours of the night, telling me of your "Home on the Range," where you play with the antelope and the skies are not cloudy all day.

I would like to ask you, if it's alright, do you ever get tired of being hunted—by cars, by predators, by me, by this world that carves paths where trees used to stand? I try not to wrap my hair around my finger or to shift my feet as I ask you how you just keep moving, weaving through it all with the kind of grace people like me will never understand?

I wonder if you feel the weight of the things this place carries at night, at least how it does for creatures like me. If there's a place where memory sticks to the air, it's here, isn't it? Or maybe that's too personal, this *is* our first time formally talking. Am I stepping out of line?

Oh, but I wonder if you remember where the forest used to be, where seldom is heard a discouraging word, before concrete sliced it all apart. Is it alright if I ask you if you remember where the trees once stood behind my house, before the apartment buildings rose from the earth one day?

I have said too much. The streetlight flickers again. You blink. Your velvet ear twitches, and your tail that has been dipped in snow flickers. Your oh-so-shiny shoes shift. I blink. You're gone. Just like that, no goodbye. Just a whisper of movement. I forgot to tell you my name, and you forgot to tell me yours. When will I see you again? Will you be here tomorrow, or maybe the next day? How will I find you again? Shall I look for you in the cracks of the sidewalk, in between the latest hours of the night?

The night breathes around me. A siren wails. A church bell rings. A bedroom light snaps off. I walk home.

Empanadas (paint chips on matboard), Sara Aparicio

KATIE PENNA

Our History and Tradition

Sometimes,
I sit and stare
and realize
how insane
I sound.

Sometimes,
I ponder and wonder
and it dawns on me
how *normal* it is
to feel this way.

It isn't right,
necessarily,
but I know there are others…breathing silently…in and out, in and out…like the beat of a heart...
because that's all one can do in this mystery pain.

I know there are others
who dream of swallowing
the moon and the stars and growing a whole tree out through their mouths, plump with ripe fruit,
yet they are forced to swallow
this dry pill,
as if they are sick.

I know there are others
being told that they are
hysterical…or *reactionary* or *aggressive* or *emotional*,
and *"it's just what happens,"*
"you'll be alright,"
and *"boys will be boys,"*

or *"lie down and all will be fine!"*
Oh, tell me, *please*, is anyone else weary of *lying*?
And they feed us the smiles, the pills,
the chocolates, and the flowers,
as if we are their little,
deranged children,
fragile with tears
and a hot, heady magma of fear.
And they feed us until we are fat
and docile as cows, grazing on their lies,
and in our quiet,
we sit and stare
and realize
how insane this shit is.

Then, oh, then we begin to bray, kicking until the next pill,
until we forget with the hope of remembering again.
That is our history and tradition.

The Unspoken Game (ink and charcoal on paper), Alleta Patterson

MADELYN TERESA ROBINSON

Anthropology of an American War Veteran

Stones, rocks, pebbles, too much of them
Languidly gnawing the seams of my pockets.

Fabric stitches demandingly unravel,
Obligating a choice.

My assemblage, enormous and diverse.
Kaleidoscopic, multicultural, contemporary.
Grey stones, brown pebbles, murky green rocks,
Muddy, freckled, textured.
Dull kitchen knives. An unforgiving butcher's cleaver.

A few artifacts dulled over the years,
Worn down by the monotonous tick, tock. Erosion.
Nevertheless, beware,
For smoothed rocks still are dangerous
If manipulated by external forces.
A dormant volcano can erupt at any moment.

Many of the boulders in my pockets remain just as sharp
As the day they first were collected.
Violent weapons, red bubbles surfacing, dripping down my wrist,
Gory, vibrant, and beautiful.

They told me to let go.
Leave the past behind.
They said it was bad for my health,
Like whiskey, cholesterol, not flossing.

Then hurried me off to a shoebox full of drugs.
Little, balding mice wearing bleached white coats
Filling stupid tiny bottles
With stupid tiny pebbles

Which are too trivial, too feeble
To dull my exotic, brave minerals.
Malleable, unable to diminish my collection, dilute my culture.

Sure, the stones weigh down my pockets,
Heavier, perhaps, as I tread the path.

Burdensome only for the beginning.
I stopped noticing the weight of it after a while…

I am comfortable carrying the extra weight; familiar and safe.
Like a bear preparing for hibernation,
Who knows how long this winter will last?

But if you empty the jewels from my pockets,
I may just f l o a t away.
The law of gravity doesn't account for the density of my rocks.

Fragments of identity
Embedded in those crystals.
The result is less whole than the sum of its parts.

For even if I could empty the stones from my pockets
Like the child's scraped knees, playing tag on pavement,
My heart will forever be marked by imprints from the gravel.

Deer Sebastian (oil on canvas), Alex Herrera

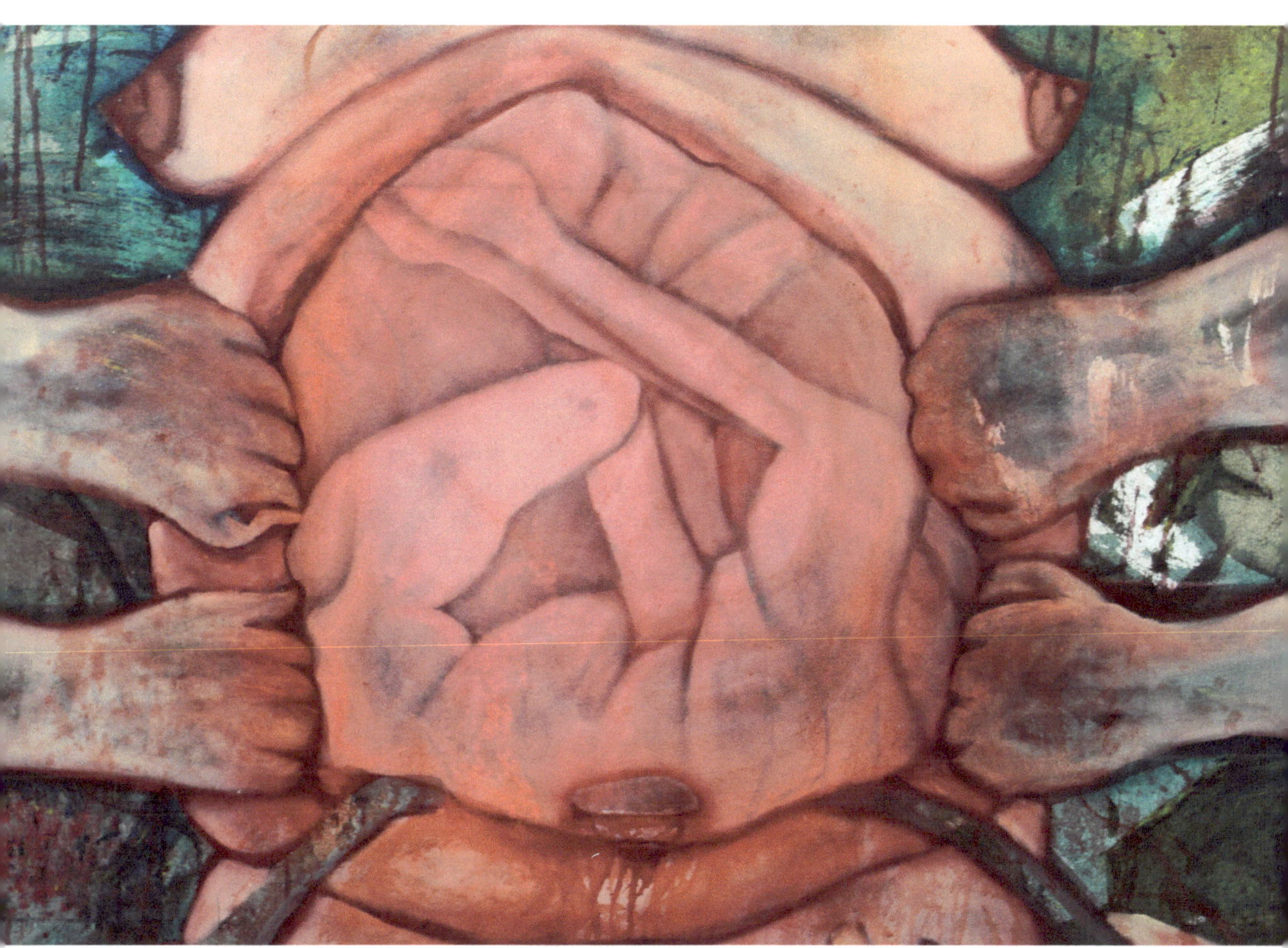

Immaculate Conception (oil on canvas), Alex Herrera

MOON KHAN

This Body, This Place

I shouldn't be left unattended at night. When I look at myself in the mirror I can see the arched point on my eyebrow that matches my mother's. I used to turn the mirror around when I had it in front of my bed. I heard it's bad luck to have it stare at you as you sleep. So I hardly look into it, especially at night. I want to feel warm. I want to be laid out across a cool metal table and inspected. I want my organs to be checked for maggots. I'm paranoid about things like slippery little flesh chowers that sneak right in. The worst part is that you wouldn't be able to do anything about it when they're eating you alive. All I can do is wait until you've disappeared.

I am unsure of what I am to you. If you see what I've built, the roof is made of chiffon that lets the air roll in. What is that to you? Is it just soft material? Did you have a desire to break it? What did you think you'd find once you got in? I am too easy to invite one in. Too easy to please and too eager to get my top off so you can start to like me again. In my house, I haven't had a visitor in almost three years—

I thought I could be the easy chick. Seventeen stupid, stupid seventeen. I think of that sunny Saturday I saw you. I should've run away until my legs gave out. I should've gone back on the train to Brooklyn and stayed there until I learned my lesson on meeting boys at Flushing Meadows Park without my elder sister's permission. I was a bad girl. I should have been punished.

When you leave me unattended at night my thoughts go unchecked—my questions go unanswered. I go to this *other* place. The same place I go when I'm writing a story.

I can hear their mouths when they kiss. Saliva stringing and pulling apart, making these obscene squishing noises that I am severely conflicted about. I hear it as I'm shifting underneath my comforter, the sound emitting from the room beside mine. It's faint, so faint that at first I thought it was the leftover shower water dripping on the floor. Then the noises became elongated, and I knew it was the product of humans. The sound of their wet and smacking skin makes me an unready bud that's been peeled open.

The sound makes me feel like I want to recoil into my shell, but I want it. I rattle the way my mug does when I turn the microwave on high. I want that feeling pounding against my skin like heavy droplets of rain. The disinhibited wanting and clashing of teeth and tongues but this time with somebody who really wants to take their time—

I remember being injected with a love so pure that I didn't need to take my medication. I remember when being good was enough.

When I lose something it takes finding something new to get it back. I lost the freedom of exhaling with ease in the presence of young men who I don't know, or understand. Last October I watched all three imaginings of the *Texas Chainsaw Massacre* films in one night and allowed it to haunt me while I slept. Leatherface slashed my stomach in half with his chainsaw. He had taken the first layer of my twenty-one-year-old skin and my coffee-stained teeth. Sally, if she was a slut instead of a virgin.

I had cut a rip in my baby lavender tank and taken two tubes of fake blood and emptied them both. Some dripped from my forehead, some over my neck, some splattered across my chest, and some smeared across my chin and cheeks like war paint. That was last year when I wanted to be scary.

This year, my roommate, a girl with disheveled blond hair and a philosophy major, assigned Halloween my favorite holiday solely based on my oversized Metallica T-shirt and the smeared mascara under my eyes.

I like Halloween for several reasons. One, I get to cover myself in as much fake blood as I please. Two, nobody can tell me I'm weird because of it. Three, I can be sexy, dress the way sexy is supposed to dress, and talk the way it's supposed to talk. Or, if I fail, I can watch other people try to look sexy. For girls it's always clothing cut just below the thigh, so you can see almost everything. A loose, but form-fitting yellow mini dress: sexy traffic controller. For guys I suppose it's a tight-fit superhero suit of some kind, like Batman: ripples indented on the abs to imitate a six-pack. Deadpool if he's not like the other guys. Or a cowboy.

Cowboys ride around on horses with pistols in their back pockets. They're like vampires who can smell the blood on me from miles away. Cowboys get turned on by the idea of conquering the already broken.

The perfect view of swaying green, right in front of me. I looked at the tall sets of wood and my fingertips grazed the fuzzy leaves. There is a humming under my skin as they tower over me, dancing crookedly. I stare at their bumping of branches, the brushing of bush. Like the brushing of an arm on an arm, young skin against young skin. Nobody understands what I mean when I point at them. *They're dancing, don't you see it?* These trees are the only place my body feels safe. We don't appreciate them enough, the pure and clean air they bring to our lungs. Call me pathetic, but I'm a tree hugger, that's right. I try to understand roughness that leaves my fingers in splinters. I look at them, the sky, then at my thigh accidentally brushing against another. I pull back suddenly, nearly trip over my feet running to the bathroom. A red solo cup spills on my foot.

I've always been afraid to cry in front of the mirror. I do it here because I've got enough liquor flowing through me to start a fire. I smooth my hair, disheveled from my American flag printed cowboy hat, blot the wet eyeliner streaks on my cheeks, and sniffle. I meant it to be ironic. A brown girl dressed like a whorish Uncle Sam.

I hear "Gimme More" blasting from the living room. *It's Britney, Bitch.*

Dance, I do. I saunter, or do what I think is saunter. I kick a leg in front of the other like a praying mantis and wave my arms around as if I am pushing them through unclean pond water. That is not sauntering, it's something of my own making because I can't stand to abide by the rules of all that is defined. I stumble drunkenly in my skimpy booty shorts and tank top, which is tight enough to squeeze my barely-there breasts together. I think I'm successfully sexy. I down what's left of my cup, licking my chin as it drips down the sides of my face.

I swear to God I can dance. My knees lower, I get to the ground with my star-spangled cowboy hat slipping off my head as post-head-shaving Britney Spears blares over the loudspeakers. That was supposed to be her comeback moment, swaying around lazily in her shimmery bra and tiny shorts lip-syncing to her own lyrics at the VMAs. She was supposed to be sexy. Instead, the tabloids called her a fat drunk.

For a second my knees dig into the sticky, liquor-covered floor. I feel the blood cells bursting and bruises forming. I have this need to be swallowed into the ground. I point outside the window, and nobody's eyes follow because here I'm a shadow, nothing. I point to the lengthy bodies of swaying and kissing greenery. *Why don't you understand? They're dancing and it's all for you.*

Was there a part of me that liked it? A sickly, poisoned stem that I'm not aware of? Was there a part of me that begged for it with my silence? Was there a part of me that was long gone from the physical plane? Was there a part of me that was wandering around, watching myself sink cowardly into the cushion under his heavy breathing, his rage-filled hands? Was there a part of me that accepted it?

Was there a part of me that could've said __?

Give me a gun, I'll shoot it. In the air, in the mirror. I'll take one of the pieces scattered on the floor, the piece that contains my left and only my left eye. You know when you look in the mirror and you stare for too long, and you start to think you're staring at a demon? Then you look away because you're scared the demon is starting to look back at you? That's what the left eye is like. I read somewhere that the mirror is hard water. In the liquid void of reflection, I'm never-ending.

You can be anyone. You're not special enough to be the sole *you*. I'm sure you wonder what I think about. This, I'm egotistic enough to be certain of. I suppose that you think about whether I feel anything at all. Most of the time, I try to appear as if I feel nothing. I try to crawl underneath my own skin as if I were born a turtle. If I were born a turtle, I'd have a shell, wouldn't I?

Some things, some people, are just made to be unmoored.

This is how they made me. Out of control. This is how I was born. I used to throw eggs from the twelfth floor of my apartment building when I was a little girl. I'd watch them hit the windshield wipers and hear the splat sound against the glass. I'd watch them nearly strike the woman on the phone in her backyard. She didn't even notice I was throwing them, so I kept going until she did. Do you want to know why? I was bored.

I went to the park that day because I was bored. The sun was refreshingly hot and bright. It looked like a yellow cast lamp under the substances, leaving a dot in my vision. I went to your house, allowed you to fondle with my breasts while I watched Jennifer Connelly grace the screen in a frilly wedding gown—because I was bored. I feigned a laugh at your mispronunciation of "Labyrinth." *Laby-rinth.* My whole life, I've been bored. I wanted something that would take me out, make my soul tumble out of a vehicle as the tires dash at a hundred miles per hour. Trying to end the boredom, I became ruined. Trying to end the boredom, I walked down the stairs, but my body stayed limp across your pull-out bed in the attic. My underwear off and my top peeled down to my waist, no tears because the spirit had already left. This is a crime scene. I come back to the site to flash photos of my blood-stained, lavender lace panties. Trying to end the boredom, I realized all I wanted was a wet paintbrush stroking my skin, coloring me yellow.

My teachers used to scold me when I went to other places. Like on top of the imaginary pink pony that I told everyone was mine. I kept going to this place. There was a shell and then black and then a portal.

Inside the portal I found that I'm in between. Nothing, therefore, everything. A little mark with unruly black hair. I sat silently in the back and I stayed in this place.

This place is where the floor is made of cool marble. I lay myself down and press my cheek on it and feel my sizzling skin turn icy. This place is my house. In my house there is a chandelier, with flames in place of crystal, and a large bathtub. The bathtub is deep. So deep that when I sink in all the way only the top of my head sticks out. I sink under the water for a minute to understand the brink of death.

The water is warm. So warm that I feel my own warmth pool between my thighs. I could come from the feeling of it sinking just beneath the first layer of skin. This is the pleasure center of the house.

I have always liked the water. At the beach I wait for the waves to pick up so they can carry me. They push me gently back to shore, where it's only up to my ankles. The nature of the ocean is gentle and motherly, it's the nature of nature that turns it rough.

In my house the bedroom is floorless. I fall into it every night. Here I am falling through images. Through my imaginary ponies. My backyard that never was. This is the death center, where I hit rock bottom.

I had a dream that I said the word. I dreamed of my thighs being felt up by a man I didn't know, and I could feel his dirty breath. It's always that one breath that's all the same. It's like a black flame they share, an insistent, parasitic desire. It happens so quickly, the shift, the flip from shining pearls to pure black. Insistent desire, the wrong kind, the soul-sucking kind, the black hole.

Whenever I go to the beach, it'll call me to submerge myself—and I will—but only up to my midriff. I'm afraid to go too deep, afraid it'll kill me. Although I recall jumping into the deep end of a swimming hole, just once, on a trip to Madagascar. I stood over the water, my cowardly reflection rippling across the body of deep blue. I held myself, shivering and damp from the afternoon swim in the shallow end. My feet slipped against the gritty, wet rock as I waited for the right moment to jump.

I had a dream of being shaken by his touch so violently that the word spilled from my mouth twice. __, __!

I know this feeling. I know because I can hold it in my hands and put myself back in that place. That place is my house. That place is outside, where you are, where you've always been. The underground warehouse raves with your friends. Late one night, you opened the chiffon ceiling. You came into my house and set the roof on fire.

I took this feeling from my womb as you watched it pulse and drip blood from my hands.

So, why won't you believe me?

You can't fill the void unless you feel the void. I stood on the edge of the rock, still waiting. The only other girl on the trip told me she'd save me if I drowned. That god, Her god, is with me. She was a six-foot-tall Mormon girl with shiny blond hair and lifeless aquamarine eyes. She told me that I have nothing to be afraid of, and welcomed me from her spot at the center of the deep end, fresh water bubbling over the rocks. She welcomed me with open arms to save myself, the same way the Lord saved her. I believed her.

Fearing the void made me think I was dying. My chest pulsing harsh and fast, the rock scraping mercilessly against my slippery feet. But it called me quietly. Welcomed me to sink or swim. I jumped. The melody of the void is a deep gurgling and rumbling that brushes gently against my eardrums. The earth is separate from this; the earth is pavement and platforms, and this is just falling, forever. For a second I thought it would keep me. It lets me feel boundlessness, lets me feel the fear of sinking, my feet never touching the floor. For a second I am suspended in the void, and the nature of the void is neutral. For a second I don't think about anything at all. For a second I've returned to my mother's womb, curled up into myself. For a second the lamplight is dim, and my little body is beside hers on my bed. She's singing me to sleep. The nature of the void is static.

I woke up in a sweat-muddled body. I woke up with the violence finally purging itself from me. The remnants of the watery, endless void still clinging to my skin like a breastfeeding infant. I woke up today unashamed.

I have brief moments of true sexiness. On the StairMaster, when I'm covered in a sheen of sweat and I'm huffing hot and moist puffs of air. Sometimes I get carried away on the steps. I put the speed on five and almost walk myself over the edge. The press machine. The one that forces your thighs to push down. Sometimes I hold them down a little longer, let it burn a little more because it makes my insides melt.

I'm in line for the girls' bathroom. The material of my mesh blouse is damp with sweat as women line up behind me, and the air grows hot and silent. I can feel them looking around. I can feel them looking at me, and I would replace the floor with knives just to know how they see me. Whether they're really seeing me, or seeing through me. The truth is they're not paying attention to me at all. They're all so focused on themselves, the mirror, their delicate hands, the loose strand of hair, and beads of sweat on their upper lips. We've been waiting in this line for a couple of minutes now. Today is the second day I have been bleeding. I want to rip my shedding uterus lining from me and feed it to the soil in my garden for roses to grow. Perfectly in season, it's nearly eighty degrees.

Somebody has been sitting in a stall for too long. We hold our breaths waiting for our turn. This is so much more painful without my music. I didn't take Tylenol for my cramps because the pressure doesn't start until around 10 a.m. I woke up at eight in the morning, when it's a delightful throbbing that feels manageable. I forgot about what happens at ten o'clock and I'm upset with myself, but I've accepted it. The stall finally flushes, and the door swings open. Swirling in the toilet bowl is my left eyeball, surrounded by the last layer of skin. The layer of slightly more youthful flesh that you liked because it was always soft and warm. I can feel her coming out of me; she plops into the toilet bowl in pieces, and I sigh in relief. My womb empties. I'm not afraid of you anymore.

God forbid a girl wear a shirt with her nipples visible through it. Sometimes I want to rebel without reason. I want you to see my nipples and the fatty tissue of my breasts bouncing because I can see how it makes you squirm. You stare at them, then look away quickly, and then look again like a toddler with no self-control. You're ashamed of how perverted they make you feel.

Covered or uncovered doesn't matter. Covered, your eyes find vulgarity in the shapes my mouth makes when they have nowhere else to go. You'd find pleasure in prodding it open if it were stapled shut. Uncovered, your eyes land on my areolas, whore first, Madonna second. I am not ashamed. Look at the body and sink in lust or swim past it as if it's nothing.

My body in this place is a copper sculpture, fogging up with cold mist from the outer air creeping in. You stare up at it when you visit and quickly get bored when you find there's nothing inside of it that you can take. Copper is a common metal, pounded into pennies and worth one cent. The body in this place is covered in thin drapery, similar to the chiffon ceiling. Nipples through the material and the V-shape between the legs are where your eyes go while a droplet of blood hits the floor between the insides of the ankles. You don't notice, and you don't care to.

There is no escaping your unraveling gaze and you're angry at me, so damn angry that staring is all you're allowed.

I can hear a girl's classical music playing through her headphones as she click-clacks on her keyboard. I'd like to wrap my body in her spirit. How can she type coherently during times like this? Is she even really typing, or trying to convince her imagined audience that she's still sane? The soft piano blasting out makes me violent with pleasure. The way it lulls me, I want to cut open my stomach and place a still chirping bluebird safely inside. So, I do. I take that bird and shove it beneath my rib cage. I'll fall asleep tonight with its noise sending hot vibrations through me until sunrise. I promise, I will be whole again.

Necrolog (10 Years) (relief print and spray paint on paper), Desislava Furber

The Forgotten House in Richmond Town (intaglio etching on paper), Alexandra Cordato

LIZA RINDELL

Cupid's Eve

When I go to parties,
My throat is filled with
Pre-knotted cherry stems,
And up my sleeve I save
A single, steel-sharpened dart.

I'll rope you into bar-stool banter
And with my soured, honeyed lips
And with my small-talk smoother than oil
Your body and your mind are safely kept
Glued down to your seat.

And as the months go by
And you start to lose your ground
I'll tell you the earth is the ceiling
Until you see it the wrong way around.

Sixteen daffodils on your table
Thirty chocolates in a box
Nineteen poems on your nightstand
—You roll your eyes when I say
I have an endless supply
In my scarlet, hollywood toolbox.

I laid a picnic for us beneath the April dogwood tree
I'll distract you with whispers of sweet nothings

And tell you: “it must be a ringing in your ears—
Because I don’t hear a thing.”

How funny that you’ll never know the irony
In my faded, yellow jacket,
When I tell you the only nests in this tree
Belong to the birds
                —Don’t look up.

I wonder why you check under your bed at night
When I’m already beneath your sheets.

LIZA RINDELL

Cordoba Canaries

Porcelain feathers with glass-jointed toes
Are tufts of white and yellow sat
Perched in the green tuliptrees
　— Our living radios.

The little bird sings: "You don't have to be sad."

Transposing us, who from their height can be
Seen shifting checked tiles carefully
Chosen, soaking, clicking
Violet for you, but blue for me.

The little bird sings: "You don't have to be sad to write."

Your wind chimes, copper, the fork tines,
Silver, borrow diamonds from the sun.
A latticework of steel-woven lilies
　— Our table.

The little bird sings: "You don't have to be sad to write a poem."

We'll use the real cloth ones tonight—
I'll fold them into puddles, stars, and sunrays for you.
Bleached arms reach like a canopy,
To shade our faces gray and blue.
Wreck the handle. Pick it up.
Fly into

The little bird sings: “You don’t have to be sad to write a poem,
but it certainly helps.”

Late Night Light (acrylic and oil on paper), Alleta Patterson

Porch Friendship

I love you
sitting on your terrace of self-forgetfulness,
like a book I can't put down.
A field of olive trees.

A letter read on a leaving train.
The tenderness of a mundane afternoon,
and the reckoning of a tempest.

I love you and that
night when we were
drinking crap wine on your balcony
stuffing bread in our mouths and talking of nothing.

I'll never forget ugly dancing to the Beatles, or when I told you
it is a privilege to know you.
And it's the truth that I would give up anything in this universe
for you to love yourself the way I love you,

because my greatest enemy is
your self-loathing
and I know that poetry would pump through your veins if you could see
the way your eyes light up at the simple mention of
Bulgaria.

Live wild and gently, please.
So that in the decades of our future,

when you're gray-haired,
and your brown eyes reveal a lifetime of adventure,

I can visit your sequestered farm of sheep
and we will talk until the sun's disk coincides with the wavering horizon.
Dance until the wine is gone, and the mountain is still.
I will tell you then, and I will tell you now,

it doesn't matter to which cosmos our souls traveled.
Our entwined pasts would have forever whispered
from the narrow gorge of time,
"I'm here, waiting, always."

live figure (oil on canvas), Jade Maracic

AMELIA WEITKNECHT

Imagination's Memoir

We once lived, her and I, I do not think there is much more of her for me left. But I'll tell you, before we go.

In the summer, the cicadas sang loud and strong. Their voices surrounded, humming through us, through thick sweet air. Through hazy pink skies. The grounds were golden. They weaved and slithered in great arching tapestries. The dancing fronds crumbled and crunched in small pink fingers. The floors were soft and green until they were not. Until they crunched under too soft feet, prickling and scratching like little claws at the back door. Until they pricked our back where our shirt rode up or our neck where our clothes did not reach.

In the summer the sky was huge. The sky was cerulean. The sky was angry and dark and hot. It rumbled over us in great purple swirls. Turning the golden of the hills to the only color we saw. Gold and purple, the purple that is almost blue, almost gray, brilliant, strong.

We saw the twinkle lights blink in the yard, moving to each other's rhythms, floating about, finding love. We danced with the floating lights, waving about little twigs of crackling light, little sparking sticks that we used to write our names into the thick of the silky blackness around us. In the summer, we laughed. We laughed for a good long time.

The air was sweet and thick, if I had to pick a word for it, it would be purple. A pale purple. Perhaps it would be periwinkle, the color of the little flowers that line the road we call God's hill. The ones nobody cared to plant, but sprouted up anyway. On that hill there was a place where we could stand, where there was nobody to either end of us. No houses peeped at us, just clouds lazing by and golden fields, whispering in endless patterns that repeated. Again. And again. We, her and I, that is, liked to go up to God's hill and sniff the honeysuckle air. We liked the small tucked away field that was green, not gold, where the thistles grew, and the purple flowers must surely have hailed from. We saw red and tanned deer standing, watching from this little field. Spying, for their barely baby-anymore fawns. We often liked to think we were one of them: in the summer.

We spent everyday together, every night. The world was one place that could be anything. Everything…

I remember a glorious, gold-gilded afternoon, where we were playing in the mountain tops, a mountain surrounded by a forest of thousand foot trees. We had been chased from our home in some tiny village by marauders and murders, savaging our entire family. Her parents were dead, her sister was dead, and everyone she had ever known and loved had left her. She was left alone to find a home in the great tree tops with some other lost little ones she had gathered up along the way. A little miscellaneous bunch of ducklings tottering about a forest. But the tree had become home, and the treetops a city. Great big forts had sprouted up with winding bridges of sycamore log and weeping willow chords. Everything was decorated with puffy cattails from the burbling streams hidden away under root.

This day, when the same black suited killers of our younger years came again, they were bit back. Fought off. Great bouts of power from our very own fists struck them down in the streets of root below. This was now our kingdom. Our great mountain to protect. We decided then, with our bunch of scruffy heroes, that we would grow old here, taking in those who passed to create a great army.

In the summer, when it got dark and the thickness of the air would become moisture on the weeds, we would have to leave the forest, our great kingdom. Our band of heroes would go off, become little ruffian kids once more, and we would retreat to the soft touches of our mama. The gentle sheets wrapped around us.

In another summer, she would forget about that great kingdom, from time to time. Every now and again we would visit it, bringing together our friendly heroes once more. But, there were many places to visit. Many places to forget. I still remember though.

One day, in another summer, we found a secret garden out past the golden tapestries, in the trees that separate the fields across the street, from the rooms with the gentle sheets and wonderful mothers. We were surrounded by chicken wire with little paper plates protecting onion and chive leafs. There was a little stream, not so much of a stream, but it wound through the grass growing very long above it. And some hidden persons had placed a dusty red-ish grate across it, no more than one good jump's width. This was a secret place, a magical place. We found so much wonder in our secret garden in the woods. It became the birthplace of many great cities, and worlds, and tragedies.

Goodness, in the summer, we always loved a great tragedy. There would be blood, the death of family, the loss of friends, burning, cracking, disgusting experimentation that would split you from hip to throat, your insides hanging out. We would challenge our tragedy, that was the wonderful part of it, we would fight it off and be greater after. We would be fraught, wake up screaming and be protected by invisible friends who were always bigger and stronger and older than us. We were loved dearly and loved back in return. But of course it was all good fun. We were saved, and in turn, we did the saving. We saved ourselves and fought with bravery and were often struck down. But yes, this was the fun of it, in our perfect cities.

Of course, we still will have such wonderful bloody romps, but now only in our dreams. We do not get lost in them so often as we once did. To me, that is the great true tragedy of her life.

In yet another summer, there was this neighbor lady who watched us. A mama, but of a different sort than ours. On those summer days it was hot, not warm. We squashed potato beetles between rocks with some other more boyish ruffians,, that were the neighbor lady's own. That day, the air did not feel as purple as before. That day, for the very first time, I felt a bit tired. The air was sluggish, and I felt crackly, and she had not seemed so happy for this adventure. But still, that night it was dark and cool and the stars had bursting lights, cracking between them, in shots of red and gold. The ruffian boys seemed not all together so bad, when we all got tossed into a world of chasing and villainy by the explosions bursting above us. In that summer, we giggled until we were sick of it. And then we went dancing in the hot steamy rain, buck-ass naked with not-so-little pink toes covered in moss and dirty stone bits. Howling our giggles. Smiles cracked our face in two, until our cheeks were so sore that we had to come up with a good sour expression to balance them again.

That summer it was still purple.

As she got bigger the summers got faster. I would flee, every now and again, when her world got so dark I couldn't breath through the thickness of air. This always happened when she would become angry, yet, I couldn't fathom what she was angry at. She would simply become boiling hot and mean.

When it was not summer, the bigger ones, like Mama but not, started to become less big. A few would snip at her in sugary ways, always making her bubble up. There were several that came and stamped out our beautiful worlds as we built them. At first, she was spitting mad but soon that faded into dullness, acceptance. They would say garbled words, I could hardly hear about the silliness of such things. She would always get on with her goings and our worlds would crumple away. This is when I would get tired again. When things always seemed too bright and then nothing at all.

It felt funny to me, as the summers passed, that the others, not bigger at all now, would say it was I who would change the world. That I would be the one to make a difference, to come up with new things. Things that they said would bring salvation, industry, and future. But then they would drag her away from me, make her do horrible, boring, silly things, all in the name of "education." But I could never figure out what she was learning. All I could see was a sat-still-girl at an empty desk, filling out the paper just the same as every other ruffian.

In the summer, the days became short. I fear I was asleep for most of them. She left our wonderful Mama and only looked back every few weeks. But for the most part, she was no longer ruffian. She was no longer a hero, or an adventurer. She sat behind her desk and that was all. That was what they taught her to be.

And hah! I would not live in a gilded tower forever. But I also would not live in a dusty corner. I'd sooner be snuffed out entirely with her only speaking to me every few years. Perhaps she returned to me any time she saw a child playing in their own perfect city, or remembered that one little bird from a forgotten special thing. I kept falling asleep, but I still loved her, and I did not want to imagine her time without me. I kept waking up, and she kept looking a little older, a little wrinkled around her eyes. She had loved and been loved now. She had lost love now. I kept feeling dust around me. We did not visit the beautiful places so often anymore, just her desk.

When I woke up, I saw the real tragedies that others faced and it was not so fun. There was bitterness in our world. The floating twinkle lights were just these little bugs that got in your hair and when they were accidentally stepped on, created a sad smear of glowing paint. There was so much all around us, but I just couldn't see it any longer.

In the summer, now that so many of those silly little worries went away, she remembers how to be a ruffian. I visit often. Not so often that she notices me, I think, wrinkled and gnarly as she is, but still. Still, every now and then we will romp around again. And how I love her so very much when we do. I have noticed that the world is brighter now when I wake up with her. There is more beauty to be seen. Silly little things are not so silly if they bring joy. So why shouldn't they matter? And why must the desk? Why should they be little? I am still here. Always.

"Do not take away the weight of joy my love." I think she's learned to hear me now, after so many summers. I think she understands the silliness it all really is.

I love you my wonderment and I do not forget our romps. I will never forget our cities, and adventures. I still notice when you come to visit me, my dearest friend, and always will.

Silly Little Forget Me Nots (oil on canvas), Amelia Weitknecht

ZOE LAVALLEE

Teeth

My father kept my baby teeth
in the top drawer of his dresser. Buried
under fabric and dust, pearls chime
against plastic. I remember
when I lost my first tooth,
I was afraid to nestle it beneath my
pillow. I did not want a dollar
in my mouth, metallic tang seeping
into my empty gum. Tissue spotted
with blood as I lose tooth after tooth until
I chew with silver dollars and spit
iron. My father's nimble
fingers slip under my hair, splayed
over little-kid sheets, and grasp
at jagged, white edges. He keeps
the treasures from my mouth, rolls
baby teeth between his fingers like
marbles. Holds the last part
of infancy, settled into the lines on his
palm. I think about how I cried when
I lost my first tooth in soft dough,
the bagel I was eating raw in my hands. I
spat the tooth onto my lap. We remember
that we never wish to lose
the first things we

grow.

Kissing Booth (acrylic on canvas), Emily Elizabeth DeRosa

ZOE LAVALLEE

To the flowers in my grandmother's garden

Why do you not smell
as sickly as you did when
my hair was braided
with pink ribbons from the Dollar
Store? Coconut lotion
infiltrates nostrils as
my grandmother plaits
my hair, tying off
the ends with rosebud satin.
The ribbons come
from the sewing kit [cookie tin] nestled
in the hutch under the boxy
television, like the one my mother
let me watch when I paired socks
on her floor. Cheap fabric
and wool. My fingers fray
with split-end thread.

My grandmother
pulls weeds from her garden. Goldenrod
hides behind swollen lupines. Tulips burst
from sticky stems and bend ever
so slightly over the marigold patch. Everything
smells like citrus and summer and little

girl evenings on a too-big boat in a too-
small bay. My grandmother's cubic
zirconium ring flashes next
to a white rose. The reflection
is skewed.

She keeps her
diamond, small and young, hidden
upstairs in the redone master. She
presses the fabrics in her closet
to her nose. Smells artificial,
counterfeit lily. Lets her body fold
into the California king, breathing
over the bay. The pink carpet my
grandparents tore up rots
somewhere. Far away. My mother
inhales purple crocuses. Perhaps
flowers die. Perhaps it is

spring.

When life gives you Lemons 1/30 (10 layer screenprint), Grace Vibal

Highway Forever

Fuck,
steel ripping into opal ribbons
drenched in orange-brown sweat,
tips melting into gooey ash pavement,
flood of my black river,
dust plumes from plastic radiator girds.
I'm close,
slow motion catastrophe and
chrome heat death,
freeway eroding vaginal walls of sand.
I love you,
as cadmium stains my palms,
forever desert double-helix,
forever pressed against your waste.

ADA BENEDICTO

My Honest Thoughts on Yukio Mishima

McDonald's is a porn theatre.
Sweet, glossy yellow bread. Bright, glossy yellow moth lights.
August walks in, orders a burger. Number sixty-seven. Thinking, this is what Mishima would
do.
I'm speaking down to the Japanese officers in Ichigaya and I'm about to kill myself. Thinking,
this is
what I would do.
Salsa falls on my menu. My eyes dart around, before I gently lower the previous page onto it.
I pass
it to the waitress. I'm sorry. I'm a fuckup.
You always need to know your name. At Starbucks I say, I don't know. Jean. Jeauww-n. Like
French.
Not here. I'm 67.
You're 67, and it tastes the exact same.
McDonald's encompasses the sun.
You're 14, and you're jerking off to Saint Sebastian, and smelling the sweet umami of a staling
burger
and
pressed against your lips, Big Mac sauce running down your thigh, it tastes the exact same.
Little yellow crown of love.
I'm sitting with Mishima and he says, I loathe the American occupation, but secretly, and I
would
never tell a soul, I love this.

Sunday Brunch

My Dad gave me
Penguin Modern Classics.
He was so proud.
Thick sludge and honestly
I ate it.
Tongue on Nietzsche
Opalescent grease
All over my hands
And everyone knew.
I told everyone
Brought them over
Eyes on me
I was so happy.
When my friend says
You're an animal
And I say no. No man.
Pouring down my lips
Stoic and cool
I'm Red 40 glow.
I'm an American.

Homunculus (clay, fabric, mixed media), Amelia Weitknecht

ELIANIZ TORRES

Budded

The flowers planted along the church's stone walls never looked a day past bloom, each of their petals as perky as they were the day before. Somehow surviving the winter winds and blistering cold. Somehow persisting through the birds that invade their sanctuary. Somehow maintaining their sculpted figure. I wonder if the sun whispers to you while he touches your face. Does he point out to you that your neck is drooping ever so slightly? Remind you that the browning rim of your petals depreciates your value, strips you of the only reason you're kept alive. How tragic it must be to exist in the constant pursuit of beauty.

Almost as if in response to my questioning, you shed, in quiet agony, another petal over my shoulder. It falls beside my palm. A failed attempt to hold onto something, rather than to be held. Suddenly I feel guilty, my hands are heavy with the blood of your stems. I wonder if you knew how much people loved to touch the parts of you that hurt. The parts that were yanked from the ground and cut down to fit better. Match the pattern of their upholstery better. Wonder if you understood you were a currency of love, a way to say *I'm thinking of you and you look lovely*. A way to apologize for a bad day, or plan for a good night. Would it change how your face fell as you aged if you did? Would you feel a sensation of peace as you died, in an unfamiliar place, hidden beside other petalless corpses mounted for decoration, all because it was in the name of love?

My mother never taught me not to pick flowers, never explained to me that you were just as alive as me. Just as alive as my baby sister. A small patch of flowers grew alongside the far fences of the softball field. After each Wednesday night, once the game had ended and my father joined us at the bleachers, his forehead dripping with salty beads of sweat, I'd run to them. Graze my little fingertips over their faces, watch them dance in the wind to the rhythm of their scented song. Awaiting permission. I wonder if you knew them the way one knows an old neighbor. Or if they are to you, as they were to me: perfect strangers. I plucked them as gently as I could muster and carried them in bunches to my mother, trying not to trap their delicate limbs between my fingers. I'd shoved them in her face with a smile so wide it showcased every missing tooth and told her I plucked them just for her. As if they grew there in that same corner every season just for her.

Maybe if she had told me then that those flowers' petals would rot away within mere hours because of what I had done you wouldn't be stuck here. In this poorly lit room, staring at the same four walls all day. Maybe we would have crossed paths differently, beneath the shade of a thousand-year-old tree, a few feet away from funny-looking mushroom heads and fallen twigs that snap when you look at them. Maybe I would have seen you, felt your petals, and understood the browning at their edges. Would've smiled softly at the sight of your shedding. Maybe then I would've realized that you were brave before I realized you were beautiful.

A Little Help From Our Friends (acrylic wire and yarn on canvas), Emily Elizabeth DeRosa

JAMES SEVEN PRESTON

The Storms

Whipping Whirling Twisting Turning
Rising Falling Pushing Pulling
Shaking Singing Clawing Crying
Jumping Falling Screaming Sinking

Wooden splinters slice flesh
The whip cracks through salty air
She holds the child close to her breast
Praying in languages they can't understand
Twisted sisters crying out in pain
Screams of fury that echo through time

She falls, shackles dragging her down
Sea devours her
The salt, her skin
The waves, her flesh
The rocks, her bones

Lightning shatters the sky
Sound from silence
Motion from stillness
A death of monotony
An escape from agony
She's falling again
And again she falls
Until the waters are red
The sea, her blood

The rain, her tears
The wind, her songs
The thunder, her rage
Homes reduced to wooden splinters
Wind whips and twists and turns
The ships hull cracks and groans
Bodies floating in murky waters
She is the storm

Where Are We Going? (photograph), Luciano DeRoberts

do it tonight (acrylic and ink on canvas), Sawyer Taylor Ramsamooj

JORDYN STINAR

Sad Grownups: A Review

Amy Stuber's debut collection, *Sad Grownups*, features seventeen short stories that traverse adulthood and explore the turbulent emotions that surface through growing up and growing older. The characters in these stories range from teens just entering adulthood to adults in the last quarter of their lives, all grappling with grief, love and connection, and aging in a constantly growing and changing atmosphere. They are beautifully written, believable as human beings and, at times, heartbreakingly relatable in their flaws and desires. I found myself laughing with these characters and feeling for them all the same. They balance one another out with their individuality and unique motivations, yet in a collection with such distinctive characters staged in various settings, Stuber seamlessly shows that we are not alone; really, we are inextricably linked.

Sad Grownups begins with "Day Hike," which revolves around a queer couple deciding whether or not they want to have children. Alice and Renee reflect on themselves and their relationship, as they walk a long trail together. Both women had decided "they were with the wrong people (men) and that being together after that would somehow lead to a better life. [Except] It hasn't worked out that way." This statement, laced with the subtle humor that Stuber incorporates within each of her stories in this collection, is a refreshing reflection in which both Alice and Renee believed they knew why they were unhappy and changed that singluar thing, but it did not change who they are as people in their relationship; they still have to work together to figure that part out. Alternating with Alice and Renee's narrative is a perspective from their author as she struggles to write the two characters' story. There is an interesting shift from the third person point of view of Alice and Renee to the first person point of view, making readers aware of the author's presence. The language provides clues of this presence in Alice and Renee's section as well with the opening lines being "Alice wants to walk on the trail, but Renee wants to wander. At least, that's what I imagine." Stuber is exceptionally talented at creating a voice outside of a story, giving it a meta aspect and making us think about fiction as it compares to reality. She does this again in "Dead Animals," beginning the story with "Take me on a journey. Make me feel something. Surprise me. Make me change. Okay. *Okay*," creating the illusion that the narrator is responding to prompts given to them in order to tell the story. This voice guides readers without telling them what to feel. The unique use of point of view allows the chance to look outside ourselves and reflect.

One of the most striking aspects of *Sad Grownups* is its emphasis on relationships. Many of the characters struggle with feelings of isolation and their want for, and lack of, human connection in the face of change and the inevitability of aging. A number of the stories, such as "Doctor Visit" or "More Fun in the New World," have characters engaging in physical relationships or having sex, however it is the non-sexual relationships that feel more intimate. In "Cinema," we follow a movie theater employee mourning the loss of her children. Stuber crafts an immersive setting as she surrounds a lonely, grieving woman with stories of love, seemingly fulfilled and contented strangers, and groups of children trick-or-treating on Halloween night. We find the main character in a time when the theater is showing a romance film, and as she watches a couple who have brought their baby to the movie, she begins to imagine her sons speaking to her. She looks for them in the groups of kids trick or treating, and when she doesn't see them thinks, "Maybe wanting it made it not happen. Maybe expecting it was the problem." At closing time, the woman crosses paths with a stranger who asks to close and walk with her. She begrudgingly gives in to her loneliness and agrees. The two begin to understand each other over a very short time, and give one another the company they were both lacking. Stories like "Cinema" and "Last Summer," in which a dying professor befriends a couple of college girls, among others in the collection, show us how human connection, even when it is new or awkward or short-lived, can be more heartfelt and intense than physical closeness. These sad grownups are afraid to interact or connect with people and the world around them, sometimes going through great lengths to disguise their effort or desire for connection. But when they allow themselves to be vulnerable, the results are significantly better than expected.

As adults we don't often refer to ourselves as "grownups" unless we are talking to children. In a collection that deals with heavy material and adult characters, it is ironic to see this phrasing. It suggests that adults can still relate to their child selves and even act as children. There are moments in the collection when adults relate to children, reflect on memories of their younger selves, or behave like children. In "More Fun in the New World" a mother and daughter go on a road trip after losing their husband and father who killed himself. The daughter is grieving, but also realizes she is angry at her father for choosing not to live. In Las Vegas, at a pool on the twenty-fifth floor and far away from the real world down below, they meet and befriend a man and his grandson. After swimming, talking, then falling asleep, the daughter wakes from a nap next to the boy who tells her "the adults" have gone off to a party. As the boy and the girl return to his suite, his grandfather and her mother, both drunk, walk to a bedroom and shut the door. The kids then also move to a bedroom. Afterwards, the girl runs away from both him and her mother and thinks, "I am suddenly nothing but angry at my parents, those giant loping children, all need and ineptitude and no restraint." The stories make us wonder: Do we ever really grow up? To what extent are parents responsible for their children growing up to also be sad grownups? Stuber creates a web of melancholic narratives that also give us hope—the stories do not judge, rather, they present their conflicts as a part of life. They suggest that it is not unusual to grieve, feel confused, make mistakes, grow old, and grow up.

Stuber's dynamic cast of characters also questions whether or not they matter as they battle with their place in the world and their relationships with those around them. We find this in sixty-year-old Heather, the protagonist of "Camp Heather" who works at a religious camp for boys. As she juggles her job and imagines what her future might look like, she thinks she "wants to wake up each morning thinking it matters." We see it in the narrator of "Doctor Visit" as the protagonist contemplates the death of family members and her relationships with her doctors. She imagines several versions of her family's death, and, after the first one, observes that "This is something I think about: mattering. As in, do we matter? It's a masturbatory thought exercise that undoes itself, as in, the sheer act of thinking about mattering is enough to remind you of the futility of your actions and thus proof you don't, in fact, matter, and why should mattering matter anyway?" In the final short story, "The Last Summer" prickly Adam Zanger contemplates his life and death. Told he has only months left of his life, despite being rather young at fifty years old, he reflects on how he has seemingly done very little with his time. He makes unlikely friends with two sorority girls, Carson and Lane, who are moving into the upstairs apartment of the house he lives in. The trio goes for a ride in Carson's boat and as Adam stares up at the sky, he thinks of the shift we all go through from childhood to adulthood. How we may go from needing our parents to needing the desire of strangers. He considers how we go through life just thinking of the unknown, saying, "So much of life is about possibility, about what is next, what place what person what food, will this or that thing disappoint your family, will you travel, will you fuck someone, what are you going to buy, what time to sleep and wake up and what job and not job and what time this and that and that and then how suddenly, all of it simply, quite simply, doesn't matter." In a more lighthearted moment Adam claims he'd like to teach classes on these feelings, sarcastically giving us titles such as "'living alone for a decade: making it work' or 'dying: nobody wants to, but here we go.'" The question of whether or not we matter seamlessly slips into each story, because it might be the most important question of all. Or maybe it is actually the least important.

"The Last Summer" is the perfect full circle conclusion to a collection that comically, devastatingly, and beautifully, provides us with perspectives on aging, grief, finding purpose, and coping with the expectations and demands of adulthood. As Adam addresses his feelings about his life and death, he grieves himself and what, and who, he will leave behind. In his short interaction with the girls his life changes and he begins to view the moments he has left in a different light. The story closes the collection movingly with this: "They sing, and it fills the car with lovely noise. The lights are a beautiful blur alongside their speeding. If he closes his eyes, it is always nighttime and summer. He can never not think of this."

MOLLIE MCMULLAN

An Interview with Amy Stuber

Amy Stuber is fiction writer currently based in Lawrence, Kansas, where she works as an editor for *Split Lip* magazine. Recently, Stuber's *Sad Grownups* was announced as a finalist for the PEN/Robert W. Bingham Prize for Debut Short Story Collection. Though *Sad Grownups* is her debut, Stuber's writing can be found in publications like *Smokelong Quarterly*, *Wigleaf*, *Cincinnati Review*, *OK Donkey*, and numerous others.

Gandy Dancer: While reading *Sad Grownups*, we were struck by how intimate and personal the collection felt. What experiences from your own life led you to writing these stories? How did you know that you needed to write this collection?

Amy Stuber: Most of the stories have some piece of truth from my life, whether it's an emotion or a place or an event. "Cinema," for example, was inspired by my own experiences with postpartum depression and my own sadness and nostalgia around my children aging out of previous versions of themselves. "Day Hike" is set in a place where I've been many times in Colorado, on a hike I've taken repeatedly. In "Doctor Visit," an ophthalmologist tells the main character she has "the tiniest little baby cataracts," and an ophthalmologist told me that exact thing. In that same story, the main character's mother is always trying to get the main character to try her coleslaw, and that has been true of my mother. But almost everything else in the story—the situations, the actual events of the story—is fiction.

Most writers I know weave little bits of their own lives into their work, so the end product is like a treasure map for people who know them, reading through and recognizing little prizes from reality. Most of these stories are about 90% fiction and 10% autobiography. Broadly, though, I think my own experiences with aging, parenting, trying to have solid adult relationships, trying to connect with people, and also questioning the direction of America, all fed into writing this book. And regarding knowing I needed to write this collection: I've always wanted to publish a book. That's probably two parts feeling compelled to write just because I enjoy it and can't seem to not do it and one part ambition.

GD: In "People's Parties," Ray makes a conscious effort to connect with her child, Bea, in spite of the abandonment she experienced from her own mother. Other children later in *Sad Grownups* are not as fortunate as Bea. How did you decide to place this story near the beginning of the collection? Can you talk more about the organization or order of your collection?

AS: I struggled with ordering this collection, and it was ordered in many different ways before my editor, Rebecca Burke, helped me see an order. I still wonder about the first story as first, though, to be honest. And I also wonder if "People's Parties" should even be here! It's a story that I turned into a novel draft a few years ago, so I really debated whether to put it into this book. In some ways, I'm not as sure it fits tonally. But in terms of theme, part of the ordering was, for me, an emotional progression from the start to finish of the book, with some of the early stories more tied up in a more adolescent emotional struggle and some of the later stories trending toward emotional maturity or if not maturity, release, if that makes sense.

When people talk about revision being a kind of endless process, I think that very much applies to the act of ordering and structuring a collection. I could definitely go back in now and make a case for rearranging!

GD: There is an abundance of humor across this collection. In *Sad Grownups*, Odon looks like a "child Rachel Maddow," and in "Doctor's Visit," the narrator says: "I wonder, *what is this life*, because I'm deep like that. No, ha, I'm really not." How necessary is humor when writing characters dealing with common issues like grief, loss, betrayal, aging, and so forth?

AS: I'm glad it felt humorous. I always worry that some of this stuff comes across as cringey. But, in life, I do tend to use humor to protect myself from emotion, and that definitely surfaces in my writing.

GD: The stories in *Sad Grownups* often handle difficult subjects, but never feel grim because the language has its own gravitational pull and intrigue. As a poet, I noticed rich phrasing like "grief striated" and "all of life is contained in a day anyway. Wake up its own little birth and sleep a death, and all of whatever in between." What kinds of things inspire and inform your writing, especially when dealing with heavier subjects?

AS: I love poetry! It's what I first wrote in college, and it's writing that I turn to repeatedly when I feel stuck with my own writing or stuck as a reader and struggling to focus on novels or collections. Poets like Diane Suess and Erika Meitner really inspired me during the period of writing some of these stories. I also really loved picking up big anthologies from grad school and flipping through them at random and letting whatever I settled on inform what I was writing. I love the poetry of the Harlem Renaissance and Modernist poetry more broadly and the Beats and confessional poets. When writing this collection's closing story, "The Last Summer," where the narrator, an adjunct literature teacher, is dying of cancer, I pulled directly from a Norton anthology into the story and let particular poems' themes feed the story's progression.

I know a lot of people feel like writing about some of these heavier issues is boring or cliche or whatever, and I've noticed a trend in the last ten years in novels toward focusing on less heavy topics: breakups, workplace drama, etc. And I very much like those books. But for my own writing, I tend to keep going back to some of these big life and death issues, kind of existential crisis things for me. Maybe I'm just really morbid! But I do get very much in my head thinking about death, dying, human cruelty, probably to a fault, and that definitely shows in what I end up writing about.

GD: Multiple characters in the collection are afraid to connect—or go to great lengths to disguise their desire for connection and love. This felt to us like the result of Covid-19, where we grew accustomed to our loneliness. Were you thinking about that as you were writing these stories?

AS: Possibly Covid related in some cases but also probably my own lifelong struggle to connect with people, to let down my guard, to allow myself to feel and give love. That feels very embarrassing to type! There's one story here, "Corvids and Their Allies," where one of the characters recognizes her own struggle with knowing how to love, and that's definitely personal to me. I think we all use various tactics to try to protect ourselves from hurt and heartbreak and vulnerability. These characters, much like myself, use humor to deflect, use isolation to protect, but still have a desire for connection. I wanted some of these stories to capture that very human tendency to shelter ourselves from anything that might be harmful.

GD: The settings in *Sad Grownups* are incredibly varied and memorable, ranging from Las Vegas to New York, a houseboat to a resort in New Mexico—to name a few. When writing a story, is setting the initial thing you establish?

AS: Sense of place is very important to me in what I read, and I'm very much inspired by nature and the natural world in what I write. It's not always the first thing, but that feeling of place definitely inspires everything I write. There are some places I've visited where I feel like I just have to write about the place because it's so beautiful and moving that I want to try to use words to recreate how it feels to be there (the desert in Utah or the headlands in Mendocino, CA). I also wanted to set a lot of stories in Lawrence, KS, where I live because I enjoyed writing about all these really familiar-to-me places and trying to show how some of these "flyover" places are interesting, unique, and beautiful in their way.

GD: In "Cinema," "More Fun in the New World," and "The Last Summer," death and dying force characters to interact with people they otherwise might not. What allows this? And how is this good for fiction?

AS: Generally, I think unexpected events and interactions are fun to read and write about. Stuff that happens at the margins of human experience mixed with average, everyday occurrences—that blend feels interesting to me as a writer. As in "The Last Summer": a dying man in a car with two college women drinking White Claws—that kind of absurdity where truly monumental life events hit up against the trivial—that's how this all tends to work in real life, and I enjoy trying to capture it in stories.

GD: A number of the stories feel meta in that the writer is either a character, or the stories seem to respond to prompts, like in the beginning of "Dead Animals," where you write: "Take me on a journey. Make me feel something. Surprise me." We'd love to hear more about your process creating *Sad Grownups'* metafictional qualities.

AS: This was the outgrowth of being bored with myself and my own writing and wanting to take a standard linear narrative and add a layer to it. Many of these stories ("Dead Animals," and "Day Hike," for examples) started as more standard narratives, and I finished them, read them, and thought they needed something else added to create texture or tension or interest. In most cases, this ended up being a kind of meta element that pushed the story to function on two levels. I'm not sure I'll do that in future work, but it was fun to play with in this book. And, for me, really having a narrative and metanarrative reflected the way we live in the world: our actual lives, the events we're involved in and with, conversations we have, and then our internal lives, often very different and sometimes detached from our actions and interactions.

Bonus Questions!

GD: Adulthood and childhood mirror one another in "More Fun in the New World" and "The Last Summer." How estranged are we from our childhood selves? How does that relationship influence your narratives?

AS: This is a big one for me! Without devolving too much into therapy speak, I do feel like we're all carting around our childhood selves and trying to reassure, parent, and save that childhood self, let it feel adept and confident and safe enough to kind of merge with our adult selves. That's so much of what this book is about.

GD: While reading, I noticed two references to Joni Mitchell: the title of "People's Parties," which is the name of a song from her *Court and Spark* album, and then her song "Carey" is also referenced in "Cinema." Are there other musicians that inspired you?

AS: I actually did this playlist[1] for the amazing "Largehearted Boy," and it speaks to all the music that inspired my writing of these stories. It's probably true for most writers so not unique to mention, but music, writing, art, nature—all inspire pretty much everything I write.

---

1 https://largeheartedboy.com/2024/10/07/amy-stubers-playlist-for-her-story-collection-sad-grownups/

NICOLE CALLAHAN

Trophic Cascade

The test is positive.

Amelia sits on her toilet lid, legs pushed up to her chest and arms wrapped around her knees. She had only looked at the test for a second. Maybe she saw it wrong. She feels her hands grip her thigh, her skin turning white as the pressure of each finger forces blood out of her capillaries. The small, animal reality of the gesture grounds her. It's her blood. Her body. Her legs prickling her fingers with stubble. For a moment, she's present in herself. Then she turns her head, glancing again at her bathroom countertop. The brilliant blue plus remains.

Amelia's mind is built for hiking through the terrain of Yellowstone, tracking cadavers and collecting numbers on the who, what, when, and where of their desiccation. Science is a discipline of productive uncertainties—the meaning and veracity of results, their applications—but those she can tolerate, even enjoy. A scientist moves towards understanding.

The ambiguities of language are less soluble. In high school, Amelia floated through English classes, her head full of cotton and barbed wire. Her teachers, looming over dense, old texts, would say there was "no right answer," which irritated her. In the few mandatory college composition and literature classes she took as an undergrad, what she perceived as a simple phrase could be an hour-long debate. Meaning appeared so open-ended there might as well not *be* meaning. Even in her taxonomy class, she felt filled with impulsive rage when she learned "fish" was not a real category of creature—fooled again by the common tongue. Language is amorphous. Slippery.

Positive: colloquially associated with optimism and goodness. Positive: denoting the presence of a condition or a disease. Wolves can test positive for sarcoptic mange; tiny mites burrowing in their skin cause relentless itching and hair loss. People can test positive for a coronavirus with crown-shaped spiky surface proteins that will latch onto their cells' receptors and destroy their lungs.

And sometimes, mammals test positive for the presence of a group of cells rapidly undergoing mitosis in their uterus. Like Amelia. That's if she's lucky and it hasn't attached itself to her fallopian tube in a life-threatening ectopic pregnancy. She shakes her head. She's catastrophizing, as her mother would say. Chances are the unwanted embryo is doing just fine.

She is the most pathetic cliché. A one-night stand with a guy she has no interest in seeing again from another grad program, a hasty condom application. A frantic trip to the drug store five weeks later. A pregnancy test.

Amelia is a scientist. Or at least, she's trying to be. As such, she never trusts an isolated result. So, she fishes another test out of the plastic bag she discarded on her bubblegum pink bath mat.

An hour and an additional trip to the store later, there are six unambiguous, positive tests sitting on her bathroom countertop. A laugh rips out of her mouth, hysterical and untimely. There is another word with a variety of meanings and usages, all applicable here.

Fuck.

She's got Topics in Biodiversity at 3 p.m. It's 2:53 by the time she's done taking all the tests, so she's got no time to process the situation. That's grad school. She clambers into her pants, jacket, and a mask before heading out the door. The walk to Lewis Hall from her graduate student housing in Nelson Story Towers is usually around ten minutes.

At a brisk pace, she manages to slip in just in time, certain that she looked *so* dignified to all the passersby as she half-ran across campus. She exhales and plops into her normal seat. She doesn't think she'd be in trouble even if she were tardy; Dr. Connie Peters never minds when her students are a bit late. Peters and her work at Yellowstone with the Wolf Project were the main reasons Amelia applied to Montana State University to begin with. Peters's focus is large ungulates, and they emailed back and forth before Amelia applied. When she got accepted, it came with funding as a research assistant under Peters while she worked towards her M.S. in Biological Sciences.

Amelia's thesis is on the behavioral dynamics of wolves. Conveniently, this makes the hours she spends categorizing ungulate carcasses in Yellowstone relevant to her own research as well. Dr. Peters's science is the science of open terrain, of dirty fingernails and things visible to the naked eye. It has a tangible quality that a laboratory lacks. Amelia and the other assistant, Macie, spend their weekends driving the hour and a half to Yellowstone, where they take notes on elk and other large ungulates' bodies for Peters. Aside from one summer course, they'll work entirely in the park when the semester ends in May.

Amelia opens her laptop. Peters nods to acknowledge her and then coughs roughly, announcing that class has begun.

"So," she starts, looking around. She balances against a large table at the front of the room, her posture the affected nonchalance shared by many professors. "What did we think?"

For class today, they listened to a podcast about the results of wolf reintroduction to Yellowstone. It was a subject with which Amelia, due to her thesis and work with Peters, was intimately familiar. On another day, she might have chimed in with her thoughts about hydrological regime changes due to wolf influence. Instead, she searches "pregnancy effects on body" in a private browser.

After a second of silence, Peters starts the conversation. "Well, since that podcast came out, I'll acknowledge wolf populations in Yellowstone have become even more of a hot topic politically, which I find interesting."

Despite the mask Connie wears, Amelia can tell she is smiling because her crow's feet deepen. "Yes, a lot of you-know-who's," she mock-whispers, meaning Republicans, "they want to increase hunting rights—*have* increased them—to take care of the wolf problem, quote unquote. Now, maybe I'm just old, but I remember the eighties and nineties. I was working at Yellowstone even then. And I'll tell you, from a scientist's perspective, we had quite a lack-of-wolf problem."

On Amelia's computer, a GIF shows an animated illustration of a baby in utero as it crowds the organs up the ribcage, collapsing them against a straining heart. The website describes how the heart rate elevates and blood volume increases thirty to fifty percent. The body swells, a balloon of blood and hormones.

Peters keeps talking. "I specialize in grazing habits and behaviors of large ungulates. Elk, deer, and the like. So, I was at Yellowstone to study them. After seventy years without wolves, the place was a wreck. The valleys were bare, overgrazed to hell. Genetic diversity dropped. No vegetation means no animals who eat that vegetation! It was just yellow-gray yuck. Here, I'll pull up my photo album."

Babies absorb the calcium in their mother's bones if they aren't offered enough through food. They kick at her sides and push down on her bladder. The websites say it begins to feel like you can't breathe around week thirty-one. Amelia's only five weeks in, but she feels the tiny gasps now—her breath hiccups as she tries to fill her lungs.

She looks up to see Peters, sleeves rolled up to her elbows, place the album under a projector to display the images all blown-up. All of this was touched on in the podcast, but she loves to repeat things with different emphasis and detail. Amelia's seen these photos half a dozen times.

"So," Peters continues. "No nesting for birds. No habitats for fish because the water started running broad and shallow. The damn aspen stopped growing up. Little twig-trees."

She flips through three photos labeled "1997," "2004," and "2020." The first shows thinning trees, long stretches of grass, and not much else. The next has thicker foliage, bushes dotting the ground. The final photo is the money shot: a rich field, full of all different vegetation and wildlife. Appropriately, it even has a lighter sky.

The worst would be after. Yes, her stomach would bear stretch marks and her bladder control would shrink, but the true worst would be when the child existed. Its demands would only grow after birth. Her life would be forfeited to service.

"So, people have a wolf problem now." Peters opines. "They say with too many wolves, there's not enough elk left for hunters. Actually, there's more elk now than there were then. No, in my mind, it's this old, European feeling—hatred of the wolf. White guy lawmaker, French peasant fearing the beast along the Seine. Potato, po-*ta*-to. It's a deep-rooted thing. If you ask me, these guys fear wolves, and they hunt them to feel power over what they're afraid of. Plain and simple."

Peters pauses, throwing her hands out like a victorious debate team captain. Silvia, the PhD candidate, raises her hand to say something about trophic cascades. From there, the discussion takes off as it always does. Amelia sits low in her seat and tries to distract herself from the pregnancy blogs by taking notes. Peters looks at her a couple of times where she'd normally speak up, but doesn't pressure her.

After they are let out, Peters goes up to her desk. "Alright?" she asks. She's the kind of gruff old academic who loves talking about her field and not much else; Amelia appreciates the attempt at concern.

"Yeah," she says. "Just tired from studying for the Qualifying Exam."

It's the second-semester requirement she's been most anxious about, so she's technically not lying. An oral examination on four areas of specialization. It's a trial by fire, and if she can't hack it, she'll be screwed. She's scheduled to speak in front of the committee on April twenty-sixth, only six days from today.

They talk for a few more minutes. Peters promises she'll be okay while Amelia's foot taps a record of every second until they wave goodbye.

Back in her apartment, she spends several hours researching her situation online. Then she paces in circles from her oven, around her kitchen table, to the window of her living room, and back. She slams her toes on the curved foot of her green loveseat and curses.

She won't do anything until she makes the call. She doesn't need to involve anyone; the miracle of remote medicine means the process will be entirely within her own home. But for whatever masochistic reason, she's decided to call her mom.

Amelia knows her mother will tell her to keep the baby. She also knows that's not what she wants to hear. Her mom is fairly liberal, so she won't say it out of moral conviction. No, the real reason is that, like many mothers, Donna Roberts sees her daughter as an extension of herself. It's not a conscious or malicious thing, but she does. She's always styled Amelia in her image. And Amelia knows Donna will want her daughter to replicate the choice she made.

When she was younger, Amelia could feel her mother's discontent. Her young brain took a tally each time her mother's busy hands passed her on to a bus driver, babysitter, or grandmother. She felt her mother exhale with each transfer. The inches between her parents radiated with repulsion, like two magnets of the same polarity being forced together. Amelia doesn't resent her because of that—far from it—she knows Donna performed motherhood with admirable diligence. Vitamins, checkups, Christmas presents, forehead kisses, all were given with absent-minded grace. Her mom offers love like it's her personal form of jury duty.

Donna is the type of woman who goes to church every Sunday, though Amelia has never once seen her read the Bible or pray in her free time. A social believer, not a private one. It was the same with her practice of motherhood.

It wasn't until Amelia was in her teens that she finally heard the story of her conception, retooled by time and affection into a 'happy' accident. It was *fate*, her mother cooed, but it kept Donna from touring with a prestigious ballet company. The pregnancy itself had been a horrendous struggle that almost killed her. For Donna, there is always some greater purpose. It's how she justifies all she's chosen to endure. Mother: a martyr for causes that only present themselves after the fact.

Now that she's older, Amelia can relate to her mother more. She's a vibrant woman to be around. There's still some awkward, unmotherly feeling between them, but it has ameliorated with time. The umbilical cord of obligation has begun to unwind. They work better as friends.

She collapses onto her loveseat and presses her top contact.

The phone rings four times before her mom picks up. "Hello?" she asks, voice robotic and echoey over the phone. "Amelia?"

"Hi, Mom," she breathes out. Her shoulders lower from where they've bunched up around her ears.

"Hey, honey. How're you doing up there?"

"Um. I-I'm alright. School's good."

"What're you not saying?" Donna cuts to the point. She can probably hear it, the faltering assurance in Amelia's voice. It's the same as when she called

Amelia out on totaling her car last year or almost failing U.S. History as a junior in high school.

"Well. Um—I don't—I hooked up with a classmate a couple of weeks ago. And I swear, Mom, we used a condom, but—"

"No," she moans. "You're pregnant."

"I'm sorry, Mom."

Her mother is quiet for a while. There is only the sound of breathing on the line. Donna must be planning out a new future for her disappointment of an only child. Drop out, come home, and get a job. Nothing fancy, just something for the baby's expenses. Amelia can stay home with them until she gets married someday to a guy with a nice house.

"What do you want to do?" her mom asks.

Visions of suburban picket fences vanish. "What?" Amelia gawks.

"What do you want to do, now that you know? Because nothing isn't an option. We've got to do something. But what, well, that's up to you."

"I," she starts, "well..."

"You've got school. You're good at it, Amelia. This science stuff."

Another deviation. Amelia has no mental map to guide her through this possibility. She can't remember her mother ever speaking to her like this. Offering nothing but support.

"And," her mother continues, "I know you like it. I think it's crazy, running around in the mountains with bears—you know it makes me worry so much—but you've always liked it. You used to turn on those nature documentaries after school, and I'd just watch you. So cute."

"I do...I do love it. I love what I do. I want to work at Yellowstone someday. I want to help conservation efforts, study the wolves there."

"And do you think you can finish school next year if there's a baby?"

"You want me to get an abortion?" Amelia shouts. She didn't mean to, but it punches out of her mouth like an accusation.

"No!" her mom insists. "Not unless you want to. It's your choice."

"But you'd be okay with that? With me choosing?"

"Of course! I've always told you I'm pro-abortion, if a woman needs one."

"No, I know. I just..." she pauses, rubbing at her face with the back of her hand. "I don't know what I thought. Thanks, Mom."

"So, you think you're gonna—"

"I'm going to, yeah. I caught it so early, I'm only five weeks."

"That's good, honey. I'm glad. Do you have money to pay for it, or do you need help?"

"No, that's okay. I've been looking into it, and there's this telehealth service I can call. They send the pills straight to me. It's less than 300 dollars."

"How much do you have saved up?" she questions. "You're not going to have to skip meals, are you?" Amelia can feel her mom staring down at her through her reading glasses, judging each coffee order and night of takeout.

"It'll be enough. I just wanted...I don't know."

Her mother gives a sigh. The small sound is different from how Amelia thought it would be. Not condescending, not disappointed. Just sad. Just tired. Amelia feels a hot prick behind her eyes, and her throat tightens. She gulps, trying to hold back tears. She hates to cry, especially in front of her mom. It feels childish.

Donna responds after a small pause. "You wanted to talk to someone. I understand. It's a difficult decision for any woman."

Amelia sobs, a loud and unexpected loss of control. She's been misunderstood. She didn't want to talk to someone. Well, not just someone. She wanted to talk to her mother. But how can she make Donna understand that?

While she cries to her mother, Amelia realizes why she called. Why she had to call. The inescapable feeling, the pressure. It was guilt. She wanted to confess to the person she was failing to become. *Sorry, Mom, that I'll get to do what you must regret not doing. Sorry, I won't sacrifice myself for someone I don't know, like you did.*

"It's okay, sweetie," Donna says, her voice warm and cajoling. Amelia hasn't heard her mother speak like this since she was six and dropped her ice cream at the county fair. "You'll be okay. You're making the right choice."

"I know," Amelia responds, her voice croaking. "Thank you. Thanks."

"Of course."

"I think I'm going to book my appointment with them now. Get it out of the way."

"That's smart," she agrees. "You were always so good with that stuff. Appointments, getting places on time. Self-motivated."

"Yeah," Amelia says. "Good thing. It helped me notice it early, too."

"It's a great thing, honey. Now, is there anything else? You sure you don't want me to send a check?"

Not with the expenses they had. Modest jobs, Dad's heart condition, and the mortgage. No, she wouldn't be another burden on their plate. "I'm fine, really. Thanks for listening."

"Any time," she assures. And Amelia can tell she means it.

They're two women who trust one another, whatever else they are.

"Thanks," she repeats, and almost goes to start her goodbye when she thinks of something. "Oh, and Mom? Please don't—"

"I won't tell your father, Ames. Don't worry."

She doesn't know why it concerns her. Her dad would've been accepting and non-judgmental. He's always been warm where her mother has been distant. Maybe he should know. She just has a compulsion, like the compulsion to call her mom, that this was something to keep between her and her mother. Now it belongs to the two of them alone.

Amelia books an appointment with Abortion on Demand for the next day. The physician she speaks to on the telehealth video is forthcoming and pleasant. She explains the service, all that they provide, and how Amelia can reach out at any time with her concerns. It's far from the nightmare movies and television make it out to be. Maybe that's because she does it in the comfort of her own shitty apartment, where protesters and religious zealots are unlikely to descend on her with last-minute guidance and condemnation. She raises her hard seltzer to the miracle of video health care that night, one of the small improvements made by the pandemic.

Abortion On Demand has next-day shipping, so the pills and the rest of the care kit arrive bright and early Friday morning. She had asked the doctor if it was okay to wait until after her exam to take them. According to her, it was.

But when she opens the box, she knows she can't wait. Something about having the life-saving medical marvels in her hand. Besides, it's the weekend, and the doctor said the cramps would only be bad for the first couple of days after she takes the second pill. She takes the first pill, mifepristone, minutes after she opens the package. Nothing much happens, and she spends the day with her textbooks.

The next day, she takes the misoprostol pill like the doctor advised. Around two hours after, when the cramps begin, she pops the anti-inflammatory they sent in her care kit, puts a heavy-flow overnight pad on, and takes a nap.

When Amelia wakes up, her mouth is dry, and her stomach is churning. She crawls out of bed, relieved that she doesn't have roommates to watch her as she lurches to the bathroom. The pad is already dark with blood, so she replaces it. She massages her stomach to relax it while she uses the bathroom. When she rises to flush, she sees a blood clot the size of her palm. It's not dangerously large, according to what the doctor said, but she gets a sudden wave of nausea and dizziness looking at it. The congealing, scarlet mass stains the porcelain red. It is a well of her fresh blood. She sits back down.

She never had a problem with blood before. Nature documentaries could be very explicit. She once wiped out while biking downhill and tore her knees open on the pavement. She whined about the pain, but the sight itself did not distress her. She'd flicked the dirt out of her open wounds without a hint of discomfort. Her mother shrieked at the sight of her, and only then did Amelia cry, more because she had upset her mom than anything.

She can barely do more than flush and rinse her hands in the sink. She's warm, probably from a slight fever. It's the worst cramping she's ever had. She knows she won't be able to study until her mind has cleared. It makes her chew her bottom lip to think of the committee staring down at her, but she also feels giddy relief. The frightening mass amidst the porcelain shows the pills have performed their essential function, their bloody miracle.

The weekend goes by in the usual haze of a mild fever. Her constant companion is the blood. She's not allowed to use tampons for seven days, and it makes handling menstruation messier than usual. It gets on her hands, it leaks through the sides of her pad to destroy two pairs of her underwear. It paints a bloody blot on her white bedsheets. It's nothing compared to a surgical abortion, but it is the heaviest period of her life. All of her symptoms are entirely normal, though. She's lucky. She feels tired and achy, but not out of control.

Her mom calls her several times, a precipitous increase from their usual once a week, and offers worry and support in equal measure.

Amelia snaps out of the mental fog on Tuesday, the morning of her Qualifying Exam. The bleeding has reduced to half of what it was in the beginning, and her mind is clear enough while she stands in front of the committee. She still gets the feeling she should've studied more when she flubs several times during the landscape ecology section. Afterward, though, Peters takes her and Macie out to lunch. It's nice. When she looks at Connie Peters, her gray hair tied back in a ponytail and her fingernails stained with dirt from collecting herb clippings on a trail she hiked that morning, Amelia imagines herself. Her future.

In another world, she says goodbye to them today over an unsweetened iced tea. Instead, she orders the diner's embarrassingly juvenile chicken tender meal deal. Macie smiles and Peters mocks her for her poor taste.

On the tenth, and what looks to be the last, day of bleeding, something historic happens. A Supreme Court decision leaks. She's making herself scrambled eggs, shuffling through the cabinet above the sink to find her pepper, when her cell phone dings.

They're going to overturn Roe v. Wade.

She laughs. She always laughs when she's nervous, at talent shows and project presentations. She feels outright skittish now, hackles raised. Then her logic kicks in, trying to curtail the panic. *Oh, you've already had yours. Oh, control will go back to the states and Montana will probably uphold choice. Oh, it's not happening yet. There's still time.* Her foot taps as she scrolls Twitter.

Women are going to die because of this. What can she do? She has class; she doesn't have time to process. That's grad school.

A nebulous sort of protest has broken out in front of the college union. On one side, a throng of clearly left-wing undergrads. On the other is a handful of people from the Students for Life Club. Amelia almost pities them for their underdog status here. They clutch at signs and stand against a mounting wave of disapproval. She's unsure why they need to protest at all. They've won, haven't they? The crusade should be over.

She's going to have to cross them to get to Lewis, and for a moment she wonders if they'll be able to sense her supposed crime. If they can smell the last spots of blood on her like police dogs sniffing for drugs.

As she walks through the crowd, she's buffeted on one side by chants of "My Body, My Choice." The other side tries to talk directly with the people passing by. One man's sign reads "Abortion is Murder." He used a blocky red font. Neither side feels like it's for her, or about her.

Amelia fiddles with the strap of her backpack as she reaches the other side of the crowd. Before she's fully passed them by, one man from the anti-choice side calls out to her, "Ma'am, would you like a pamphlet on the truth about abortion?"

Before, Amelia would've raced right past him on her way to class, avoiding eye contact the whole way. Today, she freezes in place, then turns her body as if she's receptive to him. She knows that's stupid; she knows she's opened the door for him to mow her down with a barrage of misinformation. She stops despite herself and giggles.

"I wouldn't laugh," he scolds.

Amelia stares up at him. He peels away from his crowd, taking steps towards where she stands a yard away. Her grasp on her shoulder strap tightens reflexively. He's a pasty-looking white man, lanky and not particularly muscular. He's dressed like a Sunday school teacher, with a pressed shirt and thick-rimmed glasses.

He maintains an unflappable expression and reaches into a tote bag to pull out some drivel on glossy paper. "Regardless of what others may tell you, nobody needs to have an abortion. It's not a victimless crime. There's more to it than they know," he preaches, thumbing in the direction of the pro-choice crowd.

One person from the pro-choice group gives Amelia an odd look—maybe sympathetic, maybe judgmental. They must wonder why the hell she's entertaining this conversation. She nods again, feeling like the lead detective in a sting operation. But what's the gotcha moment? *Too late, I already flushed the roughly pea-sized embryo down my toilet a week ago?* She takes the pamphlet.

"There's all sorts of studies," he continues, "on the science. When the baby can feel, hear, and think. And there's so many loving homes waiting for an infant to call their own. Babies in the womb are conscious. They are a human life. And the emotional aftereffect on would-be mothers is an unsung epidemic in our nation's history. A tragedy on top of a tragedy. It may seem frightening, but this Supreme Court decision is a good first step. It will wake people up."

Amelia highly doubts this man has read any studies on the topic, but she has a wry admiration for his commitment to the pretense of a logical approach.

"They're alive," he repeats. "They have a right to life as much as you or I. I hope you'll consider the sanctity of life today."

The sanctity of life.

"I don't care," Amelia blurts out, handing him back the pamphlet. She's harried, her hurry returning to her. She needs to get out of here. He splutters, refusing to take back his misinformation, so she drops it on the yellow grass at his feet. Some of their observers on the other side laugh at her shut down, but Amelia doesn't find it funny.

She means it. She has always been driven by evidence, but when he talked, she just kept thinking *I don't care*. Even if all the science in the world proved his claim, she wouldn't have changed her mind. She wanted her life the way she planned it. Her uninhabited body. The pseudoscience and moral grandstanding she could dismiss, but she couldn't be so unaffected by her own unflappable desire.

She feels like the kind of woman conservatives panic about on the evening news, one who would just as soon eat a baby as raise it. Vicious and unfeminine. She adjusts her backpack and walks away from both sides of protesters, continuing to class.

She passes her Qualifying Examination, though the examiners require several follow-up papers on landscape ecology. Considering her state in the week leading up to the exam, she decides to cut herself some slack. Finals also go well. She and Macie agree to sublet an apartment together near Yellowstone for the summer, as they did over winter break. They track ungulate behaviors and deaths throughout Yellowstone, log hundreds of hours hiking, and record where and when they find scat, herds, and bodies. They work with the Yellowstone Wolf Project team of volunteers and professionals, whom Amelia enjoys getting to know. One day, she hopes, she'll be in their shoes, helping students with research.

For her own thesis, she spends extra time with the volunteers and other researchers specializing in the different pack dynamics of the roughly one hundred Yellowstone wolves. Amelia goes on extra hikes alone.

Many of the wolves in Yellowstone are identified with a number and tracked with a GPS collar, and even those who aren't are recorded in the lists available online. Amelia becomes familiar enough with them to identify some individuals. She is impressed when she recognizes a particular wolf from Mollie's pack one day, and another from Phantom Lake the next.

She's on a hike, around mid-summer, with her usual supplies: a camera, clipboard, and bear spray. Macie wasn't feeling up to going this morning, period cramps keeping her down. Before, Amelia believed that women should ignore the pain. Power through. Now she knows that sometimes one must lie down in surrender with a heating pad and ibuprofen.

She walks along a stream in Junction Butte pack territory. The water is banked on either side by verdant vegetation. It's hot; even with her hair tied up, she feels her neck grow damp with sweat. She's thankful for the shade brought by a few tall trees as she hikes up a steep incline. Amelia rises until she reaches a plateau, a bright clearing with fewer trees. It gives her an open view of all the different bushes and flowers dotting the grass.

And three wolves huddled around a dark mass on the other side of the clearing.

The wind blows, bristling the gray wolf's thick and sodden fur. The juveniles, likely the adult wolf's offspring, feed on a large elk. The mother watches her pups eat, the dark brown one on her left, the midnight black one on her right.

Long, bright pink tongues lick at the fur of the elk. Amelia is far enough away that the fine details are blurry, but when the skin is sufficiently tenderized, she watches them tear at it, revealing blood and muscle tissue. She hears a slight growl as the black pup's eager munches bring it too close to its sibling, who tears at a hind leg. The brown pup snarls, nipping in displeasure, until its smaller sibling leans its head down in submission. The two find peace with the ease of children and return to the task at hand. They pull off small pieces at a time, chew with relish, and drag larger pieces a few feet away from the cadaver to consume.

Amelia doesn't recognize the trio. There are only so many possibilities of who they could be, but she hasn't memorized all the wolves yet. Either way, she feels the threat of her situation. Despite all her hiking, and these wolves being highly socialized by tourists, she feels the intimate threat they present. The group being a mother and her pups makes it even worse, as a mother will display heightened aggression to protect her young.

The animal will not risk uncertainty around her offspring.

She should record the sighting for Peters's research, but she can't move yet. Normally, she finds the bodies sans murderers.

The gray wolf begins to eat when the pups have had their fill. She moves with more precision, gnawing at a bone and tearing off larger strips than the pups were able to.

Amelia takes a few steps backward. She plans to hide behind a large tree at the edge of the clearing. She doesn't want to take her eyes off the wolves, though, and shuffles backwards inch by pained inch until she trips on something. Her backside makes a dull thud on the grass. She scrambles onto her hands and knees and crawls behind the conifer.

The gray wolf pokes her head up. Her muzzle is dark red and flaked with mud. Amelia observes clumps of fur missing from the wolf's side. She has mange, but not a bad case. It's a hot day, she feels even hotter from the exertion of her several-hour-long hike, but in that moment, her body chills. The wolf's dark black nose twitches, scents something in the air, and returns to her meal. She almost saw her.

It's nothing like the nature documentaries she used to watch. Maybe the camera work and background music do something to remove the feeling of watching a hunter at work. The sounds of tearing and squelching and the scent of blood is palpable, even from this far away. Flies swarm the carcass already, and the wolves bat them away with eager waves of their tails.

It's not a pleasant sight. It's not very "circle of life." The feast itself, the brutal and unapologetic destruction of the large ungulate, is natural, but there's no divine chorus to celebrate it.

Beneath Amelia's feet, the grassy valley extends, bursting with flora of all sorts. Under her hand, the roots of a tall conifer tree twist and reach out. In the air, she hears the chirps of birds. Feet away, a squirrel plucks berries off a thriving bush. The river she's following flows deep and straight, rife with beneficial riffle sections and pools where fish, amphibians, otters, and other animals make their home. The world around her is rich and diverse, a healthy ecosystem.

She thinks about what Silvia mentioned in class that day when she was busy googling. The trophic cascade. The ecological process of indirect interactions that revive the lower trophic levels, those smaller lives, through the reintroduction of a top predator. Bringing back the wolves brought elk, deer, and coyote populations under control. The aftereffect has been incalculable. Coyote control means more mice, and more mice mean more birds of prey, who build more nests with the vegetation spared by the lack of overgrazing.

The list goes on. From that one change, a wave of reorganization began. The world fixing itself.

Amelia isn't spiritual. She doesn't look at nature as the perfect system, far from it. Natural selection is random and cruel enough that she's always found it hard to understand the idea of intelligent design. We're all here by accident. A spontaneous series of interactions that produce the incredible functions called life. At the same time, she's not unimpressed. If anything, she thinks it means more that from its chaotic origin, life brings itself into harmony.

There's something profound in that. Her own little faith. It's a feeling, the result of chemical reactions in her brain, but it's also more than that.

It's not pretty; large teeth dig through flesh and fur. But beyond the aesthetic and understandable, it is beautiful. The blood. The cessation of life and the feeding of it. All of it important, all of it necessary for the whole.

She does not rise from where she'd fallen onto the ground. Instead, she waits on all fours, not daring to move or take her eyes away from the sight. She focuses on regulating her breath. In, out. In, out. The river to her right crackles with momentum.

Eventually, the mouths slow. First, the pups leave the carcass behind to play. They tug at one another's ears and tails while they wait for their mother to finish. Minutes later, the gray wolf's chewing and digging slows. She takes longer between each bite, sniffing and licking the elk, until she stops entirely.

They take off in the opposite direction, and Amelia sighs. She waits until they've gone far enough that she can't see or hear them, then rises to her feet. She brushes dirt off her knees and notices the green grass has stained them.

She takes out her clipboard and pen to make a record of where she found the elk. She doesn't move any closer. She thinks she can observe plenty without intruding on a space the wolves might return to.

A small splashing sound to her right makes her turn.

An elk laps at the river. Dappled sunlight through tree leaves illuminates the elk's brown fur a speckled gold. Only a dozen yards away lies the dead elk. Amelia remembers the comment Peters made that there are more elk now than before the wolves returned to Yellowstone. Even the hunted spread and grow better now. Death makes way for the living.

About the Authors

Sara Aparicio is a Fashion Institute of Technology freshman studying fine arts. Her work primarily addresses her Puerto Rican and Colombian heritage alongside studies from direct observation. Her more popular works are her paint chip and paper collages.

Ada Benedicto is a sophomore at SUNY Oswego, where she is studying writing and computer science.

Nicole Callahan graduated from SUNY Geneseo in 2021. During her time there she worked on the *Gandy Dancer* staff as a co-managing editor and also for *MiNT Magazine*. She is currently an MFA candidate at UNC Wilmington, where she works in The Publishing Laboratory and with *Lookout Books*.

Alexandra Cordato (b. 2003) is an interdisciplinary artist living and working in Staten Island, NY. She is pursuing her BFA in Fine Arts at the Fashion Institute of Technology. She has been featured in group exhibitions at SUNY Plaza in Albany, NY; Van Der Plas Gallery in New York, NY; Fashion Institute of Technology in New York, NY; Sunrise/Sunset Café in Brooklyn, NY. Cordato is anticipating graduating in 2025.

Jenna Curtis attends SUNY Oswego as an English education major and creative writing minor. If she is not in class or at work, she is curled up with any book she can find, writing poems, or playing *The Sims 4*.

Luciano DeRoberts is a sophomore at Binghamton University studying financial economics. In his free time, he plays for the rugby team and takes photos of places he visits.

Emily Elizabeth DeRosa is an eighteen-year-old mixed-media artist from Long Island, now located in Manhattan. She is a first-year student attending the Fashion Institute of Technology. Her art incorporates sketches of daily life, paintings of personal struggles and challenges, photography of the people and places she has encountered, and writing of current feelings and emotions. Emily likes to discover new ways to create art by trying out new mediums and techniques.

Emma Eager is a junior at SUNY Purchase, where she studies painting and literature. Her work has appeared in *Italics Mine*, featured as the cover of Issue 20. Her current work explores elements of the body through gesture, fluidity, and the suggestion of form on a micro- and macro- level.

Desislava Furber is a junior at SUNY at Buffalo, where they study fine art, linguistics, and German. Through their drawing, printmaking, photography, and more, Dessi explores their Bulgarian-American heritage and their experience growing up in a multicultural community. They believe that art is a powerful tool to share one's cultural background and to learn from the experiences of others.

Julia Gartley studies English literature at SUNY Geneseo. She enjoys solitude and dislikes olives.

Alex Herrera (he/they) is a senior at SUNY Purchase, where they are pursuing a BFA in fine art with a concentration in painting and drawing. He is a mixed media artist whose work explores the intersection of childhood, memory, queerness, and identity. Their paintings and performance work has been featured in their solo exhibition, Tiffany's Room (2025) and their graphic design work has been featured in the Purchase student run fashion magazine, *Gem 67*.

Magdalene Joseph, a psychology major at Monroe Community College is overjoyed to share her debut publication, "Reef is Just a Synonym for Heaven," and looks forward to continuing to develop her poetic voice.

Moon Khan is a creative nonfiction and short story writer. She enjoys incorporating fantastical elements into her work and using her background as a psychology student to explore the concepts of human nature and social conditioning.

Wrendolyn Klotzko is a poet studying education, creative writing, and English at SUNY Oswego. She is from the Adirondack Mountains of Upstate New York. She has been published by *The Great Lake Review*, *Gandy Dancer*, *BarBar*, and the *Nature State of Mind* anthology. Wrendolyn is currently the head poetry editor of the *Great Lake Review*, and after graduation she aspires to teach poetry at the collegiate level and get a cat.

Zoe LaVallee is a senior English and adolescent education major at SUNY Geneseo. She has recently been rediscovering her love of poetry, and is now struggling to stop spitting out words.

Jade Maracic is a twenty-one-year-old artist earning her BFA at the Fashion Institute of Technology. Working primarily in oil paint, her practice centers on capturing the nuances of human experience through observation and emotional depth. Her work reflects a deep interest in the everyday moments, gestures, and expressions that reveal our shared humanity.

Catie McGuire is an English major and is currently a junior at SUNY Geneseo. She originally hails from New Jersey and her preferred genre is poetry.

Natalie McKenzie is a senior studying musical theatre and creative writing at SUNY Geneseo. Whether on the stage, behind the mic, or on the page, she aspires to move an audience and tell stories that leave a positive impact. She enjoys exploring the topics of family, horses, and fantasy elements in her writing.

Grace O'Hanlon, born in Boston MA, is a rising senior at the Fashion Institute of Technology studying fashion business management with a minor in English (writing). Her work has been featured in *W27 Newspaper*, *Blush Magazine*, *PrimmaDonna Zine*, and *Clutch Magazine*. She is currently working on her first poetry collection titled, "*Daughter of an Undertaker*."

Mia Paone is a senior at SUNY Geneseo, studying sociomedical sciences with a biology minor. She is from Schenectady, New York, and lives there with her family when she is home from college. In her free time, she enjoys writing, going to the gym, doing yoga, reading, and spending time outdoors. Her favorite author is Stephen King. Mia is pursuing a career in medicine, but plans on continuing to write as a hobby.

Alleta Patterson is an artist whose work explores memory, identity, and perception through imagery and abstract forms. Blurring the lines between reality and dreams, her pieces delve into personal experiences and emotional resonance. With a focus on growth and transformation, Alleta's art invites reflection on fleeting moments and the power of art to heal and inspire self-discovery. Her creative practice bridges past and present, capturing the complexity of the human experience.

Katie Penna is a freshman at SUNY Geneseo studying English literature and music performance. She has been published previously in *Gandy Dancer* and currently serves on the E-Board of Geneseo's Creative Writing Club, where she continues to improve her craft.

James Seven Preston (he/they) is a queer, African American poet from Rochester, New York. James is a freshman at SUNY Geneseo, where he is pursuing a degree in Black & Africana studies, as well as philosophy, politics, and economics (PPE). His passion for poetry is only rivaled by his love of cooking and music, which they consider the most beautiful forms of human expression. This is their first publication.

Sawyer Taylor Ramsamooj is a freshman at SUNY Fashion Institute of Technology studying fine arts, and is a mixed media artist. She labels herself an abstract expressionist, heavily relying on her feelings to create movement on a canvas. She derives inspiration from music, emotions, and colors in nature. One of her favorite works is a piece called "Los Moscos" by Mark Bradford.

Liza Rindell is a junior at SUNY Geneseo, where she is studying to become an elementary school special education teacher. Apart from writing, she enjoys playing tennis and piano.

Madelyn Teresa Robinson is a student at SUNY Geneseo, where she studies psychology and sociomedical sciences. She is the founder and Executive Director of The Tomorrow Mission, a project to raise awareness about mental health and suicide prevention. Madelyn is also a photographer, athlete, and bookworm.

Elianiz Torres is a senior creative writing major at SUNY Geneseo. She began writing in middle school and has since discovered a deep and consuming love for poetry & non-fiction. Her writing often focuses on themes of family and womanhood.

Grace Vibal is an artist eager to branch out into the art industry. While creating, she's blessed to be surrounded by a community of inspiring artists that have influenced her entire process. Due to this, her works explore the importance of community and its role in our daily lives. While creating pieces at SUNY FIT, Vibal connects with every branch of the art world. She is hoping to bring art and community into every space she finds herself in.

Amelia Weitknecht is a second year illustration student at the Fashion Institute Of Technology. She plans to pursue a career in illustrated children's books and fine arts after college. Her artwork has been featured in the *Northampton Press*.

Luissed Yibirin (Venezuelan, b. 2001). Since she was little, she has always been very nostalgic. The immigration she has had to do has influenced several of her projects. Subtly, aspects and objects of her culture and religion are represented in her work, creating spaces between bright and opaque tones that form an atmosphere of nostalgia.

www.ingramcontent.com/pod-product-compliance
Lightning Source LLC
Chambersburg PA
CBHW041929010726
47507CB00003BA/224
9781956862126